A Match Made In Evan

Dads & Adages Book 3

Anna Sparrows

Cover design by Joe Satoria

Cover Photographer: David Wills (via CJC Photography)

Cover Model: Christopher John

Preface

A Match Made In Evan is written in Australian English (with Australian spelling). This book is a ridiculously sweet friends-to-lovers, double bi-awakening, fake dating m/m romance. I would actually describe it as a fun mix of romcom-vibes and melodrama.

Inside you will find two oblivious —but loveable— idiots, teenagers wreaking havoc, and probably too many soccer references for a non-sports-themed novel.

That said, while it is low-angst (with zero miscommunication), this book does also touch on some **potentially triggering topics**. These include: problematic behaviour and lying, traffic accidents, internalised homophobia, teen pregnancy, anxiety and self-doubt.

For international readers, I've included a glossary of some of the Australianisms inside, but I'm a little worried I've missed a few.

Glossary (non-alphabetised because I'm a rebel):
You right? = Are you all right?
Bundy = Bundaberg (in the case of 'I'll have a Bundy' it's referring to Bundaberg rum.)
NIDA = National Institute of Dramatic Art
Tradie = A slang term for a tradesman (carpenter, plumber, electrician, builder, etc.)

Brissie = Abbreviation of Brisbane (city)

Tuckshop (or Canteen) = a shop on school premises that sells snacks and lunches during school lunch breaks.

Chrissie = Abbreviation of Christmas

Gastro = A stomach bug/illness

Tosser = An insult, meaning 'wanker' or, more politely, an obnoxious jerk.

Woolies = Woolworths (a grocery store)

Chemist = a pharmacy or drug store

Pram = stroller

Nappy bag = diaper bag

Logie = Google describes it as 'an award for excellence in the Australian television industry'. I describe it as Australia's low-budget answer to the Golden Globes.

Whinging = whining/complaining

Yeah, nah = no

Nah, yeah = yes

Acknowledgments

A huge thank you to my amazing alpha readers, Megan, Erin, & Cindy. Your feedback really helped me stay on track with this one. (A bonus thank you to Cindy for giving me SPASM at the end of this book, too. I'm still giggling.)

Thanks to Christopher John/Christopher Correia for being the perfect Evan cover model, and to David Wills for taking the photo. As soon as I saw it, I said "That's Evan!"

Similarly, thanks to Joe Satoria for continuing to design fantastic covers for the *Dads & Adages* series. I love them all so much!

Finally, thank you, reader, for giving my book a chance. I really do hope you enjoy it.

Contents

Prologue

Evan

"**E**v!"

I swivel on my bar stool and grin at the guy I've been waiting for. "Jay!"

My best friend snorts and runs his hand through his lush, blond hair, sweeping the floppy fringe up and back. I swear he does that just to stir me up seeing as I am *follicly challenged*. (Read: I shave my head bald.)

"Why do you insist on shortening my name?" he asks. "It's already one syllable."

"Because all four letters of my name don't need to be shortened either?"

It's an ongoing joke between us. James insists on calling me Ev, and I, in turn, call him Jay. I'm pretty sure that if we ever revert to using one another's actual names, it'll be a cry for help.

"Careful," he jokes while sliding into the stool to my right and flagging the bartender, "or I'll shorten your name to 'Anne' again."

"That threat hasn't worked since we were twelve."

The bartender, a gorgeous buxom redhead, cocks her head at James. "What can I get you, hun?"

"A Bundy and coke, please," he answers, then slaps me on the shoulder. "He's paying, so make it a double."

"You're such a dick," there's no malice in my tone, just laughter. I push my glasses up my nose, and eye him pointedly. "You're lucky I love you, man."

We've known each other since grade four and have been thick as thieves since then. We practically grew up in each other's houses, and we've always thought of each other's families as extensions of our own. There were even a few years there where we combined our families for Christmas, but things changed once we graduated high school.

We went to separate universities —with him staying on the Gold Coast while I moved to Brisbane— and then he knocked up his girlfriend. Life changed significantly for him after that, while I continued the plan I'd set for myself: finish uni, become a Certified Practising Accountant, land a job at one of the Big Four accounting firms, and live comfortably ever after.

I'd never really planned on settling down, but I hadn't avoided it either. Of course, most of the women I'd dated over the years had pushed for more and I always found reasons not to marry or have kids. James covered the kids thing for the both of us as far as I'm concerned, considering how close we've stayed over the years.

"How's Mia?" I ask once he's settled with his drink. I adore my Goddaughter, but she recently turned fifteen and suddenly her dad and his friends aren't cool enough to hang out with anymore.

James groans. "She's *dating*."

I wince. *Uh oh.* There's no reasoning with James about his little princess. She's been the centre of his world since she was born, when her birth mother gave him full custody. I could try to argue that Mia is her own person, with autonomy and rights, but James still sees her as his little girl and not a young woman almost at adulthood. I can't exactly blame him — he put his entire life on hold to raise her, never once resenting her or begrudging his life choices. Of course she's his little princess. She's his everything.

"Please tell me you haven't threatened or maimed any teenaged boys lately," I beg lightly. "I can't afford to bail you out of jail again."

"You never actually had to bail me out," he sulks. "It was just a misunderstanding."

Poor, sleep deprived, nineteen-year-old James had let himself into his neighbour's flat by mistake after a night spent driving his colicky newborn around the suburbs to get her to sleep. His eighty-year-old neighbour —who really should have locked her front door— had called the cops when she'd discovered him passed out on her couch with the baby fast asleep in her capsule seat on the coffee table. He'd called me from the station in a panic, not wanting his parents to find out about his embarrassing mistake, mostly because he didn't want to worry them. Even though I lived over an hour and a half's drive away, I'd ditched my morning classes and come to his aid...and I've never let him live it down.

"Either way," I reply, "please tell me I don't need to call in any favours with my lawyer mates."

"I don't think finance law would help me, unless you've made other lawyerly friends?"

I roll my eyes. "Are you saying that just because I'm an accountant I only know other people in finance?"

"That's exactly what I'm saying."

Turning to face him properly, I rest my elbow on the shiny wooden bar top and arch my eyebrow. "You know, when you asked me to meet you because you had a favour to ask of me that you *absolutely* couldn't put into text or ask over the phone, I thought it would involve a lot more buttering me up and a lot less spending my money and insulting me." I study him intently as he sips at his drink, still facing forward and not looking at me. "What's going on, Jay?"

I'm concerned by the tremble in his hand, which makes the liquid inside his glass quiver and the ice cubes clack against the sides. It's been a long time since I've seen my best friend so unnerved and I don't like it.

"You know," I figure injecting a bit of humour might loosen him up a little, "short of murdering someone, I'll do pretty much anything for you. And, hey, even then, it's not a hard limit. I'll even help you hide the body if you ask nicely enough." I wait another beat and frown. "Unless you really did kill some teenage punk for dating your daughter. If that's the case, you're on your own."

James finally snorts and turns his head to look me in the eye. His smile doesn't quite reach his grey-green eyes. Instead, within them I see apprehension and uncharacteristic nerves. He licks his lips and sets his glass down on the coaster in front of him, the condensation marring the bar's logo of a deer or elk or whatever the hell it's supposed to be. Either way, the watermark obscures the antlers from view.

After hanging his head for a moment, my best friend finally turns sideways in his seat to face me directly. He takes a deep steadying breath, then says, "I need you to date me."

I blink at him, aware that I'm gaping. "Say what now?"

James lifts his glass and gulps down his drink as though fortifying himself further with the alcohol. "Ev," he pleads, "I need you to be my boyfriend. Well…my fiancé, actually, if I'm putting all my cards on the table."

And, even though we're both straight (or, at least, I think we are), I find I still can't deny my best friend anything.

Without tearing my gaze from James', I signal for the redhead to return, and I hold up my half-empty glass. "We're going to need another round." Not waiting for her response, I lift what's left of my current beverage and raise it in a faux toast. "To our impending nuptials."

Then I skol the whole thing in an eye-watering gulp.

What the actual fuck am I getting myself into now?

Chapter One

James

"Dad, have you seen my phone charger?" Mia yells from her bedroom.

Sighing, I lean back from where I'm fiddling with the coffee machine and call back, "What's the rule?"

Silence is my answer.

I swear, it was only yesterday she was tottering around on chubby toddler legs, her blonde hair in pigtails and her adoration for me more than obvious. But today she's on the cusp of sixteen, and I can't remember ever being as frustrating when I was her age.

Maybe I've spoiled her.

For her whole life, it's just been the two of us together against the world. My little princess and me. I'm not going to pretend that it's been easy, but I was pretty proud of myself for how well I've managed.

Until now.

Now, my kid rolls her eyes when I talk, assuming she really listens at all.

I miss the little girl who used to hang on my every word.

But kids grow up. My parents love to remind me that I wasn't much older than her when I became a parent myself.

I've decided they're evil, too. Like I need an extra layer of paranoia in my parenting, especially now that Mia has started dating.

Ugh.

However, that's not what I'm stressing about this morning. No, this morning's focus is on the appointment Mia and I have with a local private school. Mia's been on the waiting list to enrol for Years Eleven and Twelve since she started high school. Apparently, Winchester College has the most prestigious Performing Arts department in the state and, as an aspiring actress with her sights on NIDA, she has to get into this school or her *life is over*.

Yes, those are her words. No, I won't be arguing with her about them. She's doubled down on her studies to make the cut for Winchester, and I promised her that I would do everything in my power to help her achieve her goals. I'm all she's got, and that means I have to be her biggest supporter. Besides, what kind of shitty parent would I be to not even try when she has worked her arse off at school for the past three years?

"The rule is that things need to be put back where they belong," I mutter to myself as I head into the living room. I find the charger plugged into the wall socket closest to the recliner. There are dents in the worn beige carpet from where the chair was positioned prior to my teenager wanting to charge her phone and scroll through it at the same time. With a sigh, I pull the cable and the wall plug from the socket and head down the hallway. I don't bother to knock on the open door, just clear my throat.

Mia, who is currently on her hands and knees with her tartan-covered butt in the air, searching under her bed for the item in my hands, shoots to her feet and spins around to face me, her hair wild from her exertions. "You found it!" she cries, blue eyes lighting on the cable in my hands. She doesn't even look at me, just lunges for it.

I pull it back and *tsk*. "Seriously, Mimi, what's the rule?"

"Stop calling me that," she rolls her eyes, then folds her arms over her chest. "I'm not five anymore, Dad."

Please don't remind me.

Arching an eyebrow, I wait expectantly.

Mia huffs, then with as much put-upon teenage attitude as she can muster, drones, "Put things away where they're s'posed to go."

"And where does the charger live?"

Another eyeroll. "In the kitchen drawer." Before I can respond, she practically whines, "Can't you just buy me a spare for my room?"

"You can buy a spare for yourself."

"With what money?"

"The pocket money you earn for doing your chores."

Even though she's old enough for a part-time job now, I agreed that her studies were more important, and taking up any spare time with work seemed cruel.

She pouts. "I need a raise."

I can't help but laugh at that. "We can talk about that after this meeting. Which," I check my watch, "we're going to be late for if you're not ready to go in ten minutes."

Squawking, Mia nabs the charger from my hands and presses a kiss to my cheek. "Thanks, Dad. I'll be ready to go in five."

We make it out the door twelve minutes later, which is actually a record for us.

***

I have never felt as judged as I do in this moment. Sitting in the extremely posh school's office, it's all I can do not to twiddle my thumbs and fidget. Mia sits beside me, dressed in her current school uniform blouse and skirt, and I thought I was presentable enough in my corporate wear of black slacks and a blue business shirt, but the grey-haired woman at the desk turned her nose up at me when I told her that we were here for a pre-enrolment interview with the principal.

She sniffed haughtily and asked, "Will Miss Durant's mother be joining us?" and the look she gave me when Mia breezily told her that her mother has always been out of the picture suggested I'd already failed some kind of test.

I'm aware that there's a whole group of misinformed people out there who believe a child needs a mother and a father to be raised 'properly', whatever the fuck that means, but I've done a fan-fucking-tastic job on my own, thanks very much.

I might have been frustrated with Mia's lackadaisical approach to looking after her things this morning, but my daughter is the best thing to ever happen to me, and I am so proud of the young woman she is growing into.

She's no less well-rounded just because she was raised by a single dad. She's bright, and talented, and driven, and kind and...yeah, okay, maybe the woman behind the reception desk was judging me, the thirty-four year old single dad to a fifteen-year-old more than she was judging my kid.

But fuck that, too.

I'm a good dad. A great dad, even. I have been my child's biggest advocate and defender since before she was even born. She became my priority the moment her mother told me her period was late and I just *knew* my life was changing. I have never resented the choices I've made for Mia. I've never once regretted taking on the responsibility of sole custody. And she has wanted for nothing.

Hell, I was even prepared for teaching her about puberty and her menstrual cycle and all the things women seem to think men freak out about and can't handle. I did it all with zero freaking out, mostly because I had no other choice, but that doesn't matter.

While Mia was growing up, I played dolls and tea-parties and dress-ups with her. I let her do my makeup and paint my nails. I even wore the messy pink slashes on my fingers to work with pride.

As far as I'm concerned, Mia hasn't missed out on anything.

But the look the woman behind the desk keeps throwing my way suggests that she believes otherwise.

Great. Just great.

I would hate for Mia to miss out on this opportunity because of some ill-informed prejudice. It's bad enough that my job is more middle-class than the general populace of this school's parents, but if Mia is turned down because she doesn't have a mother, I'll—

"Mia?" A tall, stern looking woman stands at the opening to the hallway leading to the area beyond reception. Her auburn hair is secured on top of her head in a tight bun, slicked back with so much product that it almost looks like plastic.

My back straightens and I stand immediately, my anxiety at being judged overshadowed by the disturbing feeling of being in trouble and called to the principal's office.

Mia is much more casual about rising from her seat, tucking her phone neatly into the pocket of her green tartan skirt.

The stern woman's expression softens ever-so-slightly with the smile she bestows on my daughter. "Follow me, please."

I allow Mia to step in front of me, feeling the burn of the receptionist's stare on my back the entire way to the office at the far end of the hallway. We're led in through the door, and the principal shuts it behind me, then holds out her hand. "Bronwyn Michaels," she introduces herself crisply. "You must be Mister Durant."

"James, please," I say as she shakes my hand and then turns to Mia with her hand outstretched.

She really does seem friendlier as she smiles and says, "It's a pleasure to meet you, Mia."

Mia smiles back, "And you as well, Ms Michaels." Bronwyn gestures to the two timber and leather chairs in front of her desk as she makes her way to her own high-backed leather seat on the other side of the dark timber monstrosity. "Thank you for considering my application," Mia adds.

Bronwyn smiles at her again and nods, tapping her index fingers on the manila folder on the desk. "I've read your transcript and the reference letters from your teachers. You're a model student," she says, and I begin to let go of the tension in my shoulders.

Mia ducks her chin. "Thank you."

"Tell me, though, why you want to attend Winchester College. In your own words, if you please."

Mia launches into her rehearsed response to this question, citing the school's academic record, its resources and outstanding reputation, and its unmatched drama program. I sit back and watch her with pride, wondering once again just when my pigtailed toddler turned into this mature near-adult.

Of course, that's when she chooses to throw a curveball.

"...but, maybe most importantly," my daughter says, pausing dramatically as she looks my way. She pauses for effect, biting her lip and smiling sheepishly before turning back to the principal, "I know you're a proudly inclusive school."

My heart hammers. *What...?* Why would she say that? She's not coming out, is she? Here? Now? I'll love her and support her no matter what, but this moment seems—

"Which is *really* important to me," Mia continues, and her voice even wobbles, breaking my heart because *surely* she knows her sexuality is not going to make any difference to how much I love her, "because Dad is gay. Um, and engaged, actually."

Wait...*what?!*

***

"What the ever-loving fuck, Mia?" I demand once we're in the car. My fingers flex on the steering wheel, but I haven't made any move to start the engine.

"So, don't be mad, but—"

I can't help scoffing as I whip my head around to face her. "Mad? Why would I be mad? You only just *knowingly lied* to your potential new principal about *my* sexuality *and* my lack of a relationship for reasons only known to you."

And I didn't call her out on it, because I didn't want to tank her chances of getting in. If she is accepted, I'll have to explain that it was a misunderstanding...or something.

"I found out that they're doing this whole PR push on how inclusive they are," she explains. "So they're more likely to offer placements to families who make them look...well, more inclusive.

And just saying you're gay didn't feel like enough, you know? So...I made up an engagement." Widening her eyes and smiling brightly, she spreads her hands out and wiggles her fingers. "Congratulations?"

I'm torn between laughter at the absurdity of her scheme and frustration that, on some level, I can see her logic.

It scares me that I can, actually. Should my brain really be able to understand a fifteen-year-old's mental gymnastics?

Finally turning the key in the ignition, I sigh. "Well, it's not like they're going to ask me to prove it, right?"

***

Wrong. I was so very wrong.

Two days after that supremely uncomfortable meeting in the school's principal's office, they call me to request a follow-up interview. With my fiancé.

My fiancé whom my daughter invented.

My *male* fiancé whom my daughter invented.

"What am I supposed to do now?" I demand of her after explaining the situation she's gotten us into. A situation I'm aware I could have prevented if I'd called her out on her lie at the time, I know. But, sue me, I didn't want to ruin the impression she was making on the principal.

I still don't want to ruin that for her.

Because in the days since that ridiculous moment in that office, I've had a chance to think about why Mia said what she did. I agree that lying is bad, but if the school really is cherry picking enrolment applicants for purely PR reasons and not on the aptitude of the students in question, then maybe I don't feel as gross for going along with the lie.

This is one of those morally grey situations, I think, because pretending to be a minority group for benefits is bad, but using minority groups to make themselves look better is worse, right? Plus, once Mia's enrolled, I can stage a breakup with my imaginary fiancé and the whole thing is no longer an issue.

Except they want to meet my imaginary fiancé.

"Tell them he's out of the country," she shrugs.

"Well, that *would* have been the smarter option, but I panicked and said I'd talk to him when I saw him tonight."

Mia snorts. "Have all the years watching me do improv taught you nothing?"

"Uh, excuse me? I used 'yes, and', which is *why* I'm in this situation now."

My daughter chortles and even though I'm back to being frustrated at the whole problem she's created, her joy is infectious. "Ask Evan, then," she suggests simply and flops back onto the couch, rolling her wrist at me. "You're always telling me that you guys used to get into all sorts of mischief at my age. This can be like reliving your glory days, just on a bigger scale." Her eyes light up and she sits up straighter. "Actually, that's pretty genius. Because nobody knows you better than Evan, and I already think of him as my backup dad anyway..."

"Gee," I feign insult and lean forward on the kitchen counter on my elbows, propping my head on my hands, "thanks. Good to know you have a backup parent in mind."

"Oh, please. He's my Godfather. You literally named him in your will as the person I'll go to if you die before I'm eighteen."

"It sounds really morbid when you put it that way."

"It *is* really morbid," she acknowledges. "But, come on, admit it: Evan's the best choice for this."

She makes very valid points. Ev and I have known each other since we were little kids. I know everything about him and he, in turn, knows everything about me. Faking an engagement to him will be ridiculously easy. Hell, I don't even mind the idea of kissing him if it comes down to it. I mean, it would be weird because he's my best friend, but not because he's a guy. Not that I think Bronwyn Michaels is going to sit behind her desk and force us to kiss. *That* would be weird.

With our dinner simmering on the stove, I pull my phone from my pocket, acknowledging, "Fine. You're right. Now, make yourself useful and stir the risotto while I arrange to meet up with your backup dad."

Chapter Two

Evan

"**I** can't believe you're actually going through with this for me," James says as he opens his front door.

I roll my eyes. "You're my best friend. Besides, you said it's to help Mia. What kind of Godfather would I be if I said no? It's not like we're committing fraud by telling some snobby old bird that we love each other."

Hell, it's not even a lie. I do love my best friend, just not in a romantic way. People have legitimately gotten married under less auspicious circumstances, and all we're doing is pretending to be engaged for a quick school interview.

"Oh!" I add, pulling a ring box from my pocket, "Here." I shove it towards my best friend, who looks delightfully bewildered. "I thought this might help sell it." I waggle my left finger where a particularly bawdy silver ring, studded with cubic zirconia diamantes, is taking up prime real estate. "I've got one, too."

James is looking at the matching ring in the box with palpable scepticism. "These are very…"

"Shiny?" I offer.

"Cheap."

I gasp and press my ring-clad hand to my chest dramatically. "I'll have you know; I spent fifty on the pair of them."

"You were robbed."

"I was on a time-crunch."

"Evvy!" Mia appears from around the corner and flings herself at me. I catch her and squeeze her tightly. She's the only person who gets away with destroying my already short-enough name. It was adorable when she was a toddler, and it's still sweet now.

"Hey, princess," I greet her, then set her back on her feet. She looks so adult in her school uniform that a pang of something undefinable goes through my chest. She's a young woman now, not a little kid. Not that I'll ever treat her as anything less than my favourite little buddy. "You know, if you wanted me to be your dad, you just had to ask. We didn't have to go through this whole charade."

James rolls his eyes. "Ev..." he says warningly.

"Jay..." I turn it back on him.

Mia giggles and gives me another squeeze. "You guys have got this in the bag," she declares. "You already argue like an old married couple."

"We're not old, Mimi," I huff. "We're not even twenty years older than you."

She scrunches her nose. "Thanks for reminding me what Dad got up to in his teens."

James groans and pinches the bridge of his nose. "I liked it better when you didn't know what sex was."

"Ew," she protests, cringing for real, "please don't say the word." I open my mouth and she points her index finger at my nose. "You either."

"Spoilsport," I sigh.

"Anyway," Mia gives herself a shake and then grins as she looks back and forth between me and her dad, "as I was saying. You've got this."

***

Mia was right. We do got this. Have this? Whatever. The older woman with the stick lodged firmly up her butt is eating our fake relationship up.

As suspected, it's not hard to pretend to be dating —or engaged to— James. We don't even need to lie when she casually probes us with questions about how we met or, in my case, how long I've been in Mia's life. I don't actually believe she has a right to ask any of these questions, but it's no hardship to play along for Mia's sake. She has enough decorum not to ask us when we went from best friends to falling in love, so I almost feel like we don't need to lie at all.

"And when's the wedding?" Bronwyn asks brightly, right as I'm considering nudging the conversation back towards Mia, considering my fake soon-to-be stepdaughter is the actual applicant on the enrolment papers.

James and I exchange sideways glances, and I squeeze his knee before answering, "We haven't set a date. The engagement itself is still relatively new."

Still. Not. Lying.

"Well, we'd love it if you'd consider our on-campus function centre as an option for the event." She leans over the desk and winks. "We do considerably lower our rates for alumni and their families."

"Oh, well, we—" James starts, his tone already dismissive and when I squeeze his knee again, I'm a little more forceful.

"*Love* that," I cut him off. "I mean, obviously, we need to talk dates, and consider all our options, but—"

"There's actually been an opening in November. I know that's almost an entire year away, but our venue is highly sought after. The grounds make a stunning backdrop for professional wedding photos, and our usual decorators have won awards for their work three years running now." She pulls a couple of folders out from her desk drawer and slides them across the shiny tabletop towards us. "We can finalise Mia's enrolment at the same time as booking your wedding in."

James' expression darkens. "You're not suggesting that you'll only enrol Mia if—*oof!*" His head swivels between Mia on his left and me on his right. It looks like we both kicked him at the same time.

Sure, the implication that they'll only take Mia in exchange for us selling our souls to them is actually illegal (to be honest, the whole setup of discriminately selecting students based on their families' backgrounds is illegal, if it can be proven) but we are *not* ruining Mia's chance to get into her dream school. We're just not. No matter how evil said dream school might be.

"Of course Ms. Michaels isn't suggesting that, babe," I chime in before feathers can be ruffled. "She's just saying that we can do both things right now if we want to. I'm *sure* we can still arrange Mia's enrolment right now and then get back to her, or the lovely reception team, once we've had a chance to discuss dates." I shoot the now pinch-faced principal my most endearing smile. "Right?"

***

"Evvy, you are the actual best!" Mia crows when we're safely inside the confines of my car. She's slid herself into the middle spot in the backseat so she can lean between James and me as I drive. "Did you *see* her face?"

"I bet she'll be re-wording her trap for the next couple," James mutters darkly. "The nerve!" He turns in his seat to look at his daughter. I catch him frowning from the corner of my eye. "Are you sure you want to attend a school like this? One so clearly…" he rolls his wrist, searching for the right adjective.

"Evil?" I suggest. "Ethically unsound? Morally corrupt? *Snooty?*"

Mia rolls her eyes. "This is why I didn't feel bad asking you to lie to them," she justifies. "I *need* to get into NIDA, guys. This is my best shot at that."

"I think our acting was NIDA worthy," I decide. James snorts.

"Well, it's not like you had to do anything outside of our usual. Other than hold my hand or squeeze my knee, I guess."

"I would've kissed you," I shrug. "As far as men go, you're attractive enough."

Mia bursts into hysterics as James scoffs and flatly replies, "Gee, thanks."

Mia begins to babble about her plans for next year, whipping out her phone to text her friends to tell them that she got into the prestigious school, and James and I share an indulgent smile over the centre console before I focus on getting us safely back to his house.

Chapter Three

James

L ife goes back to normal for the rest of the year. Ev and I continue to catch up for beers or the odd meal at my place, but we both seem to forget about the whole fake engagement thing until I get an email confirming the details of Mia's enrolment in early January.

With the school year starting up soon, Mia and I have been rushing to get her new uniforms and books arranged, and I've paid the eye-watering tuition fees for the first semester, too. So it's a shock to read the email which requires *all* parents and guardians to attend an orientation evening. It would be easy enough to respond and let them know that I am Mia's only legal guardian, or to even lie and tell them that Evan and I broke up, but those plans are dashed when, not even five minutes after receiving the email, my phone rings. It's the school.

I debate not answering the call for a moment, but then realise that it might be about something pertinent to Mia's enrolment. Sucking it up, I press the answer icon and raise the device to my ear.

"Hello? James Durant speaking."

"Ah, Mr. Durant. This is Janelle Stevens from Winchester College. We've just sent you an email, however because we didn't have Mr. Bernardi's email address on file, I'm calling to confirm that you will both be attending the orientation evening."

"Actually—"

"We are aware that he is not legally Ms. Durant's guardian —yet— however you have listed him as an emergency contact, so it would be in everyone's best interests for him to attend."

Well, shit.

I can't say we've broken up if I want to keep him as an emergency contact, can I? Amicably broken up? Separated parents split these duties all the time, after all. Except he's not her parent, just my best friend turned (fake) fiancé, so...

"Yes, we'll both be there," I find myself agreeing, knowing that Ev won't mind.

It's one simple orientation evening, how much trouble could it cause?

***

"And, finally, we expect all parents and guardians to volunteer as chaperones for excursions on a rotating roster, in pairs." Bronwyn declares to the huddle of new parents. She's standing at the podium —there's really no better word for it— at the front of the hall and staring down at us all imperiously.

"What about single parents?" a harried woman, who introduced herself earlier as Marta, asks. The expression on her face mirrors the emotions swirling in my gut.

Over the course of this evening, we parents have been given the grand tour of the school's admittedly gorgeous grounds, while being regaled with expectations on how our children will comport themselves both on campus and outside it. Even when they're not wearing the uniform. Additionally, we have been told how we, as Winchester College parents, are expected to behave as well. Every single situation —from fundraisers to awards nights, and to excursions— has a list of requirements a mile long.

Is it too late to pull Mia out? Does she really need this dressed up, stuffy prison in order to get into NIDA?

Bronwyn's stern expression pinches. I can't tell if she's attempting to appear sympathetic to Marta's situation, or if she's irritated by it. My money is on the latter, but she feigns a simper. "Well, surely you have a friend or a colleague who will be willing to assist you," she answers.

At my side, Ev makes a sound of complaint at the back of his throat. I clamp my hand on his thigh and squeeze it, offering a subtle shake of my head. Which he promptly ignores.

"Not all single parents are that lucky," he chirps.

Bronwyn's beady eyes shift to us. The look on her face now says 'I knew you would be trouble makers'. She's disliked us since we managed to enrol Mia without agreeing to get married at the school function centre.

Talk about ignoring conflict of interest laws!

"I beg your pardon, Mister Bernardi?"

"Take James, for example," he makes a show of sitting back in his seat casually, even while I'm cursing him for drawing *everyone's* attention to me. "I've been his best friend since we were kids, but I haven't always been available to help with Mia. I'm still not always available, and he works so hard that he doesn't have much of a social backup. His parents don't live close enough to step in, and I've met his colleagues: I wouldn't ask them to look after a potted plant, let alone a kid."

There's a chuckle from the row behind us. Closing my eyes, I silently beg for death.

Evan's death, to be precise.

"Well," Bronwyn sniffs dismissively, "it seems simple enough to me. Either Mister Durant prioritises Miss Durant's schooling and everything that entails, or he should consider withdrawing her enrolment and sending her to a school more suitable for his own schedule."

I have to clamp my hand down on Evan's thigh, digging my fingers into his flesh through the layer of dark cotton, to remind him not to fuck this up for Mia. "It's fine," I speak up, using a firmer tone than necessary, mostly for my best friend's sake. "Evan and I will be able to make it work. Won't we, sweetheart?"

Placing his hand over my own, he squeezes it a bit more tightly than is strictly necessary. "Of course, babe. But," his expression turns genuinely sympathetic as he looks over to Marta, "because I know how difficult things were for you before we got together, maybe we should take Marta's spots, too."

She blinks suspiciously moist eyes back in our direction, her relief more than evident. "Really? Oh, I can't thank you enough. If I didn't have an eleven-year-old at home, too…"

"We'd love to, wouldn't we, Jay?"

I know this is my punishment for not allowing him to bring Bronwyn down a peg or two, and I really do feel for Marta, as well. From our brief introduction earlier, her son desperately wants to attend Winchester so he can access their IT and programming classes. Like Mia, he has apparently dedicated himself to his studies in order to get accepted, and it would suck to see a kid suffer because his mother had no other option.

"Of course," I smile warmly, and Bronwyn lets out a sound of irritation.

She forces a smile and nods. "Noted. Ms. Davies—"

"Mrs," Marta corrects her with a bit of steel in her voice. I decide that I really like this woman, and the casual fondness is compounded by sympathy when she adds, "my husband died, Ms. Michaels, and I still consider myself married."

The air in the room takes on a decidedly uncomfortable feeling after her declaration, and Ev leans over whisper, "We're adopting her," into my ear. His breath ghosts over me, eliciting goosebumps over my skin, but I ignore that in preference of paying attention to his words.

Affection swells inside me. Ev's such a softie, even if he can be a pain in the arse sometimes. Already planning on getting Marta's number so we can communicate about school issues behind Bronwyn Michaels' back, I nod. "I'm way ahead of you, bud."

It seems like this school —and its principal— will be quite the challenge, and having as many allies as possible will be our only way to survive the next two years.

It's not until I've gotten home and I've crashed on the couch with a beer in hand, processing everything that happened, that I realise I've started to include Evan in those thoughts.

Our only way to survive the next two years, I'd told myself. Not *my* only way. *Ours.*

I guess I'm coming to accept the semi-permanence of our charade.

It's funny, though, because something about that makes me uneasy, and I've never been uneasy about Ev before. Well, not since I was a teenager.

Chapter Four

Evan

"You know soccer isn't a contact sport," I tell my teammate, Connor, as I bandage his ankle.

We've been playing together on the same social indoor soccer team for the past few years, after another teammate, Jack, invited him to join us. At the time, Connor was dating Jack's dad, and I hadn't known what to think of that. Not because he's gay or anything dumb like that, but would it make things weird if Jack's dad broke up with the guy? At worst, we'd be down a player. At best, things would be guaranteed to be weird between him and Jack. But I needn't have worried: Connor ended up engaged to Jack's dad, and he has stuck with the team and has also become someone I'd even go as far as to call a friend.

Connor doesn't give off the kind of vibes that suggest he's into sports in general. He's an events coordinator by trade, and a bit more effeminate than most of the guys on the team. But he's fast on the pitch, and surprisingly brutal for a guy with a build so slim.

He scoffs. "It was a bad tackle. I rolled it as I went for it."

"You're lucky it didn't break," Jack —the polar opposite of Connor, with broad shoulders and huge, tattooed biceps— squats to inspect my first aid work. He's a fireman, so I suppose he's got more training in this kind of thing than I do. His American accent sounds so much smoother than ours when he adds, "Dad's going to lose his shit when he realises you're hurt."

"It's just a fucking sprain," Connor snipes back at him. "I'll ice it for a couple of hours and it'll be right as rain."

"Uh-huh. You know what Dad's like. You're spending at least a week on the couch."

"Oh no," Connor deadpans, "however will I cope?"

Jack arches a dark eyebrow at him. "Aren't you supposed to be going suit shopping this week? You're the wedding planner—"

"Events coordinator," Connor interrupts him.

"Sure. Anyway, you're the one who is supposed to be on top of all that shit, not me."

"Maybe it's your parent-y responsibleness kicking in," Connor suggests playfully. "Wrangling your twins" —who, at three-years-old, only recently appeared as a *huge* surprise to Jack— "is forcing your brain to join the rest of us grown-ups in being organised."

"That would be Leo doing the bulk of the organising," Jack admits, referring to his live-in nanny. "He's the organised one. He's got a proper routine with the boys and everything."

"It's almost like it's his job," I joke, lamely. Then I look at Connor. "Can you walk like this?"

Jack and I help him to his feet and, after a wobbly second, he manages to limp around. "Like I said, it's just a sprain. And," he adds, pointing a finger at Jack, "before you go getting any ideas, it's my left foot, so I can drive myself home." Before Jack can protest,

Connor points at my left hand, arching an eyebrow. "I didn't realise you were married."

"Oh." I blink down at the shiny monstrosity on my ring finger, surprised to see it still there. I joined James at the school earlier this afternoon as part of our rostered parenting duties, assisting with set up for the school disco. At least we weren't on the list to chaperone the dance itself.

After doing our bit, I came straight here, got changed into my soccer kit, and completely forgot I was still wearing my gaudy fake engagement ring. It's funny how used to wearing it I have become over the past few months.

Chuckling, I wave my ring-clad hand dismissively. "Not married. It's a long story."

"Well, colour me intrigued..." Connor leans in, eyes glinting with curiosity and amusement. "Anything that starts with 'it's a long story' is usually a lot of fun."

I can't exactly say he's wrong. Nevertheless, it's not something I really want to share with people I play soccer with semi-regularly. Especially not an actual gay man who might take offence at what James and I are doing.

Because I can admit it: pretending to be a gay couple to exploit the school's ridiculous PR scheme is *definitely* dodgy.

Then again, is it really that bad, considering the school's gross attempt to use minority groups to make themselves seem more inclusive than they really are?

Two wrongs don't make a right, a voice in my head chides.

Fine. The voice is right. It *is* that bad.

"I promise I'll tell you at some point," I answer him, hoping that will be the end of the discussion. "But, for now, if you're okay, I'm going to head back out there and see if we can salvage this game."

When I came off the pitch to help, it left us down a player, and I can see Brett getting increasingly frustrated at the lack of support from the other guys on the team. He's scowling, and even his dark man-bun seems to be wobbling ominously. (He takes his soccer very seriously, even if we are a social team who only play twice a month.)

With only twelve minutes of play left, I take my position on the pitch.

"Connor okay?" Brett asks, his dark eyes tracking the movement of the ball from one of the other team's players to another.

"Yeah. Just a sprain."

"Good." He nods, then barrels towards the other team's striker, determination etched on his face.

With some fancy footwork, he takes possession of the ball and then starts running it back up the pitch, towards the goal. He passes it to me, and I send it off to Hank, who takes a shot. Unfortunately, the goalie lunges and deflects the shot, but then Brett is suddenly in the right spot to intercept the deflection and kick it to the other side of the goal.

We all cheer and then set up for the goalie to resume play again.

When the final whistle blows, I'm panting and sweaty, and grinning broadly. I enjoy playing regardless of whether we win or lose, but close games like this one —especially where we walk away the victors— are always the most fun.

Plus, this beats running on a treadmill or jogging down the esplanade any day of the week.

"See you in two weeks?" Brett checks after he guzzles his second bottle of water for the night. His long hair is coming free from his bun, sticking to his red face in sweaty strands.

I'm kind of glad I'm bald. That looks uncomfortable and irritating.

"Sure," I nod. "But I can't do the game after that. I've been roped in to chaperoning my goddaughter's overnight excursion to Brissie that day. It's a musical theatre trip." I smile, thinking of how excited Mia is to go and see a performance of Wicked with her drama class. "How bad can five fifteen and sixteen-year-olds be?"

Brett blinks at me, then guffaws. "Oh, *mate*," he wipes tears of laughter from his eyes after doubling over. He's still trying to catch his breath. "I'd rather take my chances with a herd of three-year-olds."

"I've got two of them if you're volunteering," Jack jokes, shouldering both his and Connor's sports bags.

"I wasn't," Brett deadpans. Then he looks back at me. "My sister's in her early twenties now, but my parents used to make me and my mates keep an eye on her when she was that age…and I'm pretty sure it scared half the guys off the idea of ever having kids, or at least daughters."

"Don't you have a kid?" I cock my head, and he nods.

"Yeah, but Tom's six and he's easy going enough. Plus, his mum has him half the time, which makes it easier. That said, I am dreading his teenage years." He shudders dramatically.

"These are theatre kids," I wave him off. "Hardly the type to cause trouble."

***

Oh, past-Evan, you sweet summer child.

Theatre kids, it turns out, are *fiends*. They're loud and quirky and shameless. Their antics got us kicked out of Grill'd. If I wasn't so worried about James' blood pressure, I might actually have been impressed by the young hellions.

"Guys," I cajole as I herd our group (which consists of Mia, two other girls, a boy, and a non-binary kid) through the winding, bougainvillea-covered path through Southbank parklands towards the Queensland Performing Arts Centre, "we're going to need you to calm down. If you get kicked out of the show, I'm almost certain we'll all get kicked out of the school as well."

There are two other groups here with us tonight, but thankfully neither of those groups chose to eat at Grill'd with us. I get the feeling the other parents —in particular, the snobbish older couple who delighted in telling us they were both surgeons— would leap on any excuse to land us in hot water with Bronwyn.

"As if we'd ruin the show," Darcy sounds scandalised, widening their bright green eyes at me in horror. "That's, like, the worst thing any actor could do to another."

"Sabotage," Joey agrees solemnly. "We might be anarchists, Mister Bernardi, but we're not monsters."

Anarchists. Jesus. This coming from the kid attending the exclusive private school on the Gold Coast.

Were James and I ever this obnoxious as teenagers?

"He's going to destroy the establishment...while driving Daddy's Mercedes," James leans in and whispers into my ear, making me snort.

"His dad drives a Tesla, actually," I murmur back.

James tilts his head back and cackles, and I feel my usual surge of warmth and pride at having gotten my usually-too-serious best friend to laugh so vibrantly.

Joey makes a swooning sound and I look over to find him smiling widely at us, his hands folded over his chest. "I want that when I'm old," he declares.

"I'm thirty-five," I argue with a frown, feeling very much offended. Pushing my glasses back up my nose again, I add, "I'm not *old*."

Joey, the smug little turd, just shrugs. "It's almost two decades older than me. So, old."

"Jay, if I dump him in the river with the sharks, can you back me up and say he jumped?"

The other four kids giggle and Joey rolls his eyes. "I was just complimenting your relationship." The sadness that flickers over his face momentarily, only to be replaced by his usual smugness, gives me pause. I actually feel a bit uncomfortable and guilty, especially when he nonchalantly adds, "I don't get to see many gay couples IRL, y'know?"

Well, shit.

It's on the tip of my tongue to tell this kid James and I aren't like that when I realise that, yeah, we are. As far as the kid can know, anyway. And I'm hit with a terrible feeling that we're *faking it* while this kid is probably struggling with being a hormonal sixteen-year-old *and* whatever is going on with his sexuality on top of that.

James and I were privileged with our upbringings. We both liked girls, so we didn't need to look anywhere special for representation of the way either of us felt. Nobody ever questioned us about whether we were sure we were straight, it was just assumed that we were, like it was the default setting. We didn't really have social media the way kids these days do, either, so we could disconnect from any shitty peers once we were home.

James must feel the same way, because he clears his throat and awkwardly says, "That'll change once you've got a bit more freedom, I'm sure."

"As long as I move out of home, sure," Joey agrees. "Dad's under the impression that, if I hang out with enough girls, I'll change my mind about them. He's an idiot."

"You're not wrong—*ow!*" I rub my arm, where Jay just pinched it.

"We don't talk smack about people's parents," he says. "Especially *to* their kid."

"Who says 'talk smack'?" Darcy laughs, while Mia goes pink and complains about how embarrassing we are.

One of the others, Rose, just shrugs and tells Joey, "If you need a beard for the formal next year, I'll do it. It'll get Mum off my back about why I haven't got any interest in boys." She looks at me and James and adds, "I don't have any interest in *anyone*. I just want to dance. And sing."

And, suddenly, I realise that this is a pretty decent group of kids after all.

They're just a bit like gremlins and shouldn't be fed in public.

Chapter Five

James

"Oh my God," I collapse onto the queen-sized hotel bed next to Evan, scrubbing my palms over my face, "who knew that getting five teenagers to go to sleep in their own beds would take more effort than putting a colicky newborn to bed?"

Our room is between the room Darcy is sharing with Joey, and the room allocated to the girls. We've been listening to the doors opening and closing and the kids running between the two for hours.

I'm torn between relief that Mia is settling in and making friends, and exhaustion at having to try and control their antics. We have an early train to catch in the morning, and I also don't want to have to face the ire of the principal or other parents if I return their kids all rumpled and sleep deprived.

"Well, I never really had to do the newborn thing, so this is eye-opening," Ev says, then yawns. "Fuck," he adds, "remember when we could stay up all night and seem rested the next day? It's not even midnight and I'm buggered."

I fold the covers back and try not to groan as I finally relax into the mattress. "Maybe Joey was right. Maybe we are old."

"Bite your tongue," he grumbles, then carefully removes his glasses and folds them, setting them on the nightstand. I feel a pang of something undefinable at that. I like it when he wears his glasses instead of contacts, but it's not as if I'm not used to seeing him without them. He points his finger at me, shaking me from that random thought. "I was still a night owl until you roped me into co-parenting. This is your fault."

I can hear the teasing in his words, which is the only reason my guilt at making him continue this charade doesn't come bubbling back to the surface. Honestly, I don't think I could have handled the demands of this school without him. Having a partner to handle all the parenting stuff has not only been a novel experience, but it has taken a huge weight from my shoulders. A weight I didn't even know was that bad until I got the opportunity to share it.

"I really do appreciate this," I still tell him, even though I know he was being playful.

Suddenly, it hits me how lonely I've been these past sixteen years. Ev's always been there for me if I asked, but I've never really tried to share any of my responsibilities as a dad. Now? I can't imagine not having him by my side through any of this.

Gah. I'm getting maudlin.

I'm overtired.

After leaning over to switch off the lamp on the bedside table, plunging the room into darkness, I hear him chuckle.

"Does this remind you of sleepovers when we were kids?" he asks softly.

It's not hard to reminisce, to remember years of sleeping in the same bed, or in sleeping bags on the hard ground inside a tent in his backyard. It does make me a little sad that I can't remember the last time we had a sleepover — only that one day we never had any again. I can't help but think that if we had known our last one was going to be the last, we would have made it memorable somehow.

Unsure why I'm so intent on upsetting myself with such silly thoughts, I force a laugh, "We don't have a metric tonne of lollies or chips right now."

"Pity. I could go some M&Ms."

"*Mmm.* Maltesers."

"Great. Now I want chocolate. This is also your fault."

Stuck somewhere between a laugh and a huff of irritation, I roll onto my side, facing away from him. "Go to sleep, you child."

***

It's been *years* since I last woke up wrapped in someone else's arms. That's not an exaggeration, either. I've had flings and hookups over the years, but I haven't been in a serious enough relationship that I've slept overnight in a woman's bed.

So it is a little jarring to wake up being smothered by a lean, masculine octopus.

Sometime in the middle of the night, I must have rolled back over and directly into my best friend's embrace. He's got me tucked right up under his chin, his bearded jaw resting on top of my head while his arms are tightly wrapped around my torso. Our legs are intertwined, with one of his hooked over my hip.

And his morning wood is pressing into the side of my stomach, while mine —which is *far* too happy to have any kind of human contact outside of my own hand— is nestled into the crease of his thigh. It should not feel as good as it does. It shouldn't.

Not only is Evan a man, he's my best friend.

My dick is only acting this way because he's sick of being neglected for so long.

I'm still considering the best way to extricate myself from this situation when Ev makes a cute, almost feline chirping sound and stretches, simultaneously tightening his hold on my upper body while arching his back and grinding his swelling cock into my soft abdomen.

I can feel the moment his brain engages —right around the same time I'm afraid I'm going to lose the last hold I have on my sanity and start rutting into him— because he tenses and then laughs.

"Well," he says, letting go of me and flopping backwards, not at all embarrassed by the tenting in his boxers, "*this* reminds me of grade nine, for sure."

My cheeks flame, and I grab my pillow and plonk it over my erection. "We made a pact not to talk about that."

Ev turns his head lazily to face me, his expression one of pure amusement. I've always been a little jealous of how easily he seems to take everything in stride, like nothing ever fazes him. "It's been over twenty years, Jay. We were fourteen. Wet dreams happen a lot during puberty."

I squirm and squeeze my eyes shut. I can't admit, not even now, that while *he* might have had a wet dream when we were sharing a bed as teenagers, I had been fully conscious of the fact that I was about to come from him grinding against me in my sleep. Then I had come, and he had woken up, and I had been so embarrassed and distraught that he'd agreed that we would *never* speak about it.

"Okay, okay," he laughs and backs off, literally climbing out of his side of the bed, which I only know because the mattress bounces with his movement, "I'll stick to the pact." I crack an eye open to watch him pulling fresh clothes out of his overnight bag. "I'm gonna shower." He glances down at my pillow and smirks. "Unless you need to deal with that first?"

"Shut up and fuck off," I respond without any heat. "Worry about your own...situation."

"That's what the shower's for," he acknowledges easily, then ducks into the ensuite.

My heart hammers as I hear the water run, and for some strange reason I can't stop thinking about the fact that he's probably jerking off in there. He's left the door open to let the steam circulate —because he hates trying to dry off in a humid bathroom, something I learned during out first ever sleepover when we were kids— and my stomach does a funny flip to think that I could just lean around the corner and...what the actual fuck am I thinking?

The shock of realising that I'm contemplating spying on my best friend as he jerks off is enough to make my own erection wilt.

It has to be because I'm projecting all my feelings about finally having someone to share the load —*Wrong word! Weight! Share the weight!* — of parenting, right? Especially when it's someone I have such a history with, who I love like family.

That's got to be it. My brain is finally cracking under the strain of the past few months. Years. Whatever.

By the time Ev emerges from the bathroom, I'm calm and collected, and I'm back to feeling like my usual self, no inappropriate, unexpected thoughts in sight.

At least this will be the last time we have to share a bed for a while.

Chapter Six

Evan

"How did we end up having to do the entire leadership camp?" James mutters with irritation as we walk towards the very fancy charter bus waiting in the school's parking lot. "We *just* did the musical thing like three weeks ago."

"This was Marta's rostered event," I reply. Jay stops walking and I turn to find him gaping at me.

"This is *so* Bronwyn Michaels punishing us for being nice people."

"I mean," I can't help snickering, "we *are* lying to them. Maybe it's karma."

The thing is, it still doesn't really feel like a lie. James and I might not be romantically involved, but we have always lived in each other's back pockets. I love him, I love his kid, and spending time with him is not a hardship. If anything, having an excuse to hang out with my best friend all the time is kind of cool. It takes me back to our youth, and I'm actually a little sad that, when all this is over, our lives will go back to the way they were before. Plus, being a stepdad has been kind of neat, not that I've had to do any *real* parenting. But, yeah — this whole experience has felt *right*.

I mean, sure, I'm starting to get a little strung-out without sex —we both agreed that it would be risky for our Tinder profiles to be active during this charade— but I have porn and a fantastic imagination. At worst case, I can head out of town and try my luck picking someone up in person, like we did during our good old uni days. It might be fun to see if I've still got the charm.

And yet...that idea doesn't sound appealing.

Weird.

Maybe being in my mid-thirties means my libido is finally withering away? Or I'm becoming mature or something ridiculous like that?

"What are you smirking at?" Jay's question has me blinking as we step up to the assembled group in front of the bus. Another bus has pulled in behind the first one, just as fancy-looking and shiny.

"Just thinking about how much I enjoy this," I answer honestly, and he arches a blond eyebrow at me.

"Really? You enjoy having to ask for time off work to be a parent to someone else's kid?"

"I've loved her like my own since she was born," I shrug. "And I never take leave. My boss is actually happy. I think she's afraid that I'm going to bankrupt them if I resign."

My buildup of accrued annual leave *might* be the reason they've implemented a new 'take at least two weeks of your leave every year' clause into all the new starters' contracts. If I do ever quit —not that I have any reason to— the payout would probably be eyewatering at this point. Especially to my penny-pinching boss. There's a reason I privately refer to her as Mr. Krabs behind her back.

We're within earshot of the rest of the group now, so Jay just chuckles and nudges my shoulder with his own. Lowly, he says, "I appreciate it."

"I know."

***

"Hi Mister Bernardi," Joey says cheerily as he plonks himself down on the plush seat in front of the pair James and I snagged on the bus, "Mister Durant."

"Hey, Joey," we reply in unison, and I don't know about Jay, but I've grown kind of fond of the kid. "How's school treating you?" I ask as he settles into his seat.

Joey turns to squish his face in between the two seats so he can look at us. "Pretty good. They're casting the musical next week. We're doing *Guys and Dolls*. I auditioned for Nathan Detroit, but I'd be okay with Sky Masterson, too."

I don't know any of these names, but apparently Jay does because he tentatively asks, "Aren't they both traditionally baritones? Not that I've heard you sing, but I just assumed..."

"Yeah, okay, I *am* more of a tenor," Joey's expression pinches. "But I want to be a lead, and Nicely-Nicely Johnson is only a supporting role. And" —he sighs heavily— "I know that *every role is important* and all that BS, but...this is my second-last chance to get a lead role in a school production, you know?"

"It might happen," I put in my two cents' worth. "I'm rooting for you, kid."

"Which would be more helpful if you were one of the teachers making the decisions, but...thank you."

Another kid, one I can't name, comes and takes the seat beside him, effectively ending our conversation. James nudges me and I catch his grin out of the corner of my eye.

"What?" I ask.

"You're such a softie," he murmurs back.

"He's a good kid," I justify, unable to explain any more than that. After the drama excursion, his words about seeing our 'relationship' as something to covet —as well as the admission that his parents aren't wholly supportive of his identity— have played on my mind.

"He's come a long way from shark food, then?"

It might be the guilt about lying to him, but I feel like he deserves a more supportive role model than the ones he has at home.

"I dunno," I muse wryly, "he could still become chum."

Joey's face comes into view between his seat and his companion's. He rolls his eyes. "I hate you both."

I grin back at him, then at James. "And balance has been restored to the universe."

Chapter Seven

James

The first two nights of the leadership camp are relatively uneventful. The camp itself is located just across the New South Wales border, in the hinterland, and the activities for the kids have ranged from trust-building exercises to physical stuff like high ropes, abseiling and kayaking. They've all been so exhausted by the end of the day that, after dinners served in the camp cafeteria, they've all crashed by curfew without any pranks or cabin swapping.

On the third and final night, though, someone must have broken out the sugar because the teenagers are all wired.

"Come on, Mister D," Rose cajoles with a whine, "come do a campfire night with us. We're going to roast marshmallows and tell ghost stories."

"Yeah, and we're not allowed to do it without supervision," Mia adds, widening her big, blue eyes in the same way that wrapped me around her finger when she was just a baby. "Please, Dad? It's a teambuilding exercise. And it's our last night."

Rose nods. "Plus Mister Martins said they'll extend curfew for an hour to do it."

Given that I have done all the same physically taxing things as the kids and I am twice their age and nowhere near as fit, I was really looking forward to crashing in the uncomfortable queen-sized bed allocated to me and Evan as the chaperones for the teenagers of B Block.

Also, I want it on record that my enthusiasm for bedtime has nothing to do with how much I enjoy waking up wrapped in someone else's arms, even if that someone is my best friend and not a lover. It doesn't. I swear it. Because that would be sad, wouldn't it?

"Guys," I begin, leaning into my best 'stern dad' voice, "I—"

"Hope someone else is supplying the marshmallows," Ev appears from out of nowhere, slinging his arm around my shoulder. I lean into the embrace because to lean away would give away our ruse. (And definitely not because I'm soaking up any and all physical affection like a sponge.)

The kids in front of me cheer. Mia grabs my hand and tugs me back up the hill —seriously, why is the bonfire area uphill?— thanking me profusely.

"Don't thank me," I tell her, "thank Ev."

"Thanks, Evvy," she beams at him. I can't see it so much as hear it, seeing as night has settled in and the only light around us is either the scattered solar lights dimly illuminating our path up the forested hill, or the slivers of moonlight spilling in between the overhanging tree branches.

"Yeah, well, campfire nights are the best," Ev's voice comes from somewhere not-too-far behind me. I can hear the smile in his tone, too. "I wasn't gonna miss out."

Except I'm missing out on snuggling, I think petulantly, and then almost fall over my own feet when I realise exactly what I just thought.

It's one thing to admit that I like waking up in someone's arms when we have unconsciously drifted together during the night. It's something completely different to actively think about snuggling someone.

Not just someone — Evan.

My best friend.

I'm embarrassed by that. Not because he's a man, but because he's my best friend, and I'm so touch-starved that I'm sulking about missing his cuddles like I'm a five-year-old.

Nevertheless, it doesn't stop me from feeling that way.

Maybe I need to break our agreement and get on Tinder.

My stomach twists with guilt, which I can't quite pinpoint the source of. It must be just the idea of breaking a promise we made —a promise made with Mia's enrolment in mind— because why else would I feel bad for wanting to hook up with someone for a night?

***

"Mister D?"

I open my eyes groggily, wondering when I dozed off. There's just something about the smell and crackle of a fire that I find relaxing. Add to that the warmth drifting on the cool evening breeze, and I was doomed from the start.

"Hmm?" I ask, looking around for the rest of our group. I find them on the other side of the bonfire, and I'm not sure how to interpret the strange flutter in my chest when Ev catches my eye through the flames and winks at me.

"Mister B made everyone sit over there so you could nap," Joey tells me, settling onto the plastic outdoor chair beside mine. "But it's almost curfew, so I volunteered to wake you up."

"Right." I yawn and try to get my brain to re-engage. "Mia didn't want to?"

Joey laughs and shakes his head, a lock of light brown hair falling into his eyes. He brushes it back as he says, "She and Mister B both said you're super grumpy when you get woken up." His smile turns soft and wistful, and he looks towards the middle of the fire. "What's it like?"

"What's what like?"

"Any of it. All of it. Having a boyfriend. Kissing a boy. Fuc—"

"Stop there," I hold out my hand, glaring at him. "You are sixteen. You shouldn't be..." He arches an eyebrow, and I think back to being sixteen and sigh. "Fine. But I'm not comfortable talking about sex with you."

Or anyone. But especially not a sixteen-year-old.

I mean, having the safe sex talk with Mia was hard enough, and that was as clinical as I could possibly make it. This kid wants me to tell him how much I enjoy sex —with *Evan*, which I haven't actually had— and that's not only awkward, but inappropriate.

Still, I can't help my curiosity. "You've never kissed anyone?"

His cheeks are pink and he's resolutely avoiding my gaze, staring into the fire as he shrugs.

"You're only sixteen," I murmur. "You've got years ahead of you."

"You remember being my age, right? All I can think about is" —I clear my throat and he rolls his eyes— "*guys*. And I don't really have anyone else to talk to about it. Like, there's the girls, but they don't really get where I'm coming from, even if we are checking out the same people. And my parents..." His little scoff is heartbreaking. I never want Mia to feel that way about me. *Or Evan.* "So, yeah. I just...I hoped..."

My brain flashes back to being a teenager. To the angst and hormones and frustration bubbling beneath my skin.

To jerking off in Evan's bed as he moaned in his sleep...

I try not to cringe at that memory. It's resurfaced a lot over the past few weeks, making me squirm inside. We promised we'd never talk about it, mostly because Ev believed —and still believes— that we both just had wet dreams, uncontrollable and driven by our stupid, rampant hormones.

He was the only boy I ever thought of that way.

After that, I focused on girls. I *liked* girls. I still like girls. Women. That's never changed. Over the years, I put what happened that night down as an anomaly.

But if I can use the experience to help this kid now, maybe I can start to reconcile it in my mind. Maybe it can become something good, not just something I'm a little ashamed of.

I find myself nodding and telling him, "My first kiss was...awkward. It was a first for both of us, so it was all tongues and weird neck angles and..." I laugh, cringing at how disappointed she and I both were when we parted. "It was *bad*. I thought, y'know, it would be like on movies and TV, but...yeah, nah. Terrible. So don't go into anything expecting fireworks and magic, okay? It takes a bit of experience to get there. And chemistry."

I've enjoyed kissing some girlfriends and hookups more than others. I've enjoyed sex with some more than others, too. I put that down to chemistry and comfort levels.

"But with Mister B? You've got the chemistry, right?"

My heart speeds up at the question, *thump-thump-thumping* so quickly and loudly that I'm surprised he can't hear it. I don't want to lie to this kid, but I also don't want to burst his bubble, either. "We've been best friends for decades," I answer vaguely. "We love each other, so it's different."

"How'd you know?"

Thump-thump-thump-thump.

"Know what?"

"That you love him."

Thump-thump-thump-thump.

"I've always loved him." It's a confession which resonates deep inside me, making my stomach twist again, because it's not a lie, but it's also not what he's asking.

"I mean, how did you go from best friends to being *in* love?"

Thump-thump-thump-thump.

"I—"

"All right, curfew time!" the lead teacher on the trip, Mr. Martins, blares through his trusty loudspeaker, saving me from either lying to Joey or confessing to our ruse. There are four little bonfires set up around the clearing, and teenage groans ring out around us. "You have fifteen minutes to use the facilities and get your butts in your designated cabins. Parents and teachers will be conducting their checks and there will be consequences for anyone breaking the rules."

"I guess we should get everyone down and in bed," I push to my feet and head towards the rest of our group with Joey hot on my heels.

"But you didn't answer," he protests.

"Answer what?" Ev asks, taking up a spot at my side.

"I asked how you went from being best friends to being in love," Joey tells him as I'm ushering our group to walk down the path in front of us, feeling more like a sheepdog than a chaperone. I've done the headcount twice, and I call out a reminder for them to follow the lights on the path and walk carefully, studiously ignoring Evan's eyes on me.

"Well," Ev replies easily, slinging his arm around my shoulders and squeezing, "I've always loved him."

"That's what he said," Joey sighs, "but I meant…how'd you go from best mates to—"

"Mating?" Evan suggests, and I jab my elbow into his ribs. "Ow!"

"He's *sixteen*, Ev."

"We were both thinking and saying *way* worse stuff at that age. Hell, we were *doing*—"

"*Eww*," Mia chimes in from just ahead of us, thankfully cutting Ev off. "I don't need to hear that."

"Then don't eavesdrop," Evan sasses back.

"And watch where you're walking," I remind her.

In the moonlight, I watch her roll her eyes before she turns back to concentrating on making it back down the hill in one piece.

"So…?" Joey prompts.

"He's like a dog with a bone," I mutter, then hold up my index finger, "No bone, boner, or boning jokes."

"Damn it," Ev huffs. "You're no fun."

"No, I don't want to get in trouble for being inappropriate with the children." I scrunch up my nose. "Wait. That sounded wrong."

Joey's laughter is loud and infectious, if Evan's response is anything to go by. "*So* wrong, Mister D," he agrees through wheezing laughter. "Mia, why didn't you tell us how funny your dads are?"

"Because they're embarrassing, not funny," she calls over her shoulder.

"Take that back!" Evan demands. "*I* am hilarious."

"Dear God, you're just as bad as the kids," I tell him.

"But seriously," Joey chimes in again, "how did you go from buddies to fu—*uh*—snuggle buddies?"

His words only make me think about how much I enjoy cuddling my best friend.

Thump-thump-thump-thump.

"Well," Evan shrugs, oblivious to my hitching breath, "it was kind of gradual, I guess? One day we just...connected...had a moment...*whatever*, and it felt...*right*."

The strangest surge of emotion wells up inside me, bringing tears to my eyes and a longing that I just can't comprehend. I swallow and clear my throat, blinking back the moisture, thankful for the darkness I was cursing on our earlier walk up.

"Chemistry and comfort, then," Joey says as I have my moment. "Like you said earlier, Mister D."

"Yeah," my reply comes out a little strangled and I clear my throat again. Chemistry and comfort. Funny how I never thought of having those with Ev before. But I guess it's not a lie. We *do* have those things. "That's exactly it."

"Well, damn," he laments as he keeps walking. "I don't think Tristan and I have those things."

"He's straight," Mia calls back over her shoulder, and Joey huffs. "Trust you to know that."

Mia stops for a moment to glare at him. "Shut up."

My ears perk up as my eyes narrow, and Evan gives me a squeeze. "Don't," he warns in my ear, his breath making me shiver like it always does. "She's allowed to have some secrets." Raising his voice, he says, "Keep moving. We've got ten minutes to get you all in and out of the loos and into bed."

"I like it when you're all authoritative," I tease him, letting him know I'll drop the topic of Mia and *Tristan* for now.

"I'll remember that," he replies playfully.

Chapter Eight

Evan

"Will you stop moving?" James grumbles as I sigh and roll over for what has to be the hundredth time tonight. It wobbles the entire mattress, but thankfully the bed isn't squeaking like the one in the hotel we stayed in a few weeks back.

"Sorry," I murmur. "Go back to sleep."

"That implies I was asleep to begin with," he chuckles. Then the mattress wobbles as he sits up, propping his back against the solid, timber headboard. "What's up?"

"I dunno," I answer, and it comes out mildly irritable. "I'm just…restless."

I can't quite pinpoint why. I've felt antsy ever since the bonfire earlier tonight. It's like something is niggling at the back of my brain, but I really can't put words to the feeling.

"Did you have too many marshmallows?" James asks teasingly, in the same sort of tone he used to use with Mia when she was little. It makes me smile.

"Fuck off, I can handle my sugar just fine."

"Uh huh. My memories of Mia's eighth birthday say differently."

"You *dared* me to eat that cake."

"Not the whole thing!"

"Yeah, well, that's not what I heard at the time."

On top of the lollies I'd consumed, and the litre of soft drink, I'd wound up throwing it all up and feeling like shit for days. I still blame him for the miscommunication.

"So..." he cocks his head, "what's wrong, then? If it's not the sugar, I mean."

Giving up all pretence of trying to sleep, I sit up next to him. We're both fully-grown men, with him a bit broader in the shoulders and thicker in the middle than me, and we take up the bulk of the space of the queen bed. It really does make me think fondly of all our youthful sleepovers, like I'm reclaiming an old part of our friendship which we've lost over the years.

"I don't know," this time my answer is almost a whine. "I'm just...*keyed up*, I guess."

"Keyed up?" Jay repeats cautiously, and his tone is a little strained. "Like...horny?"

My dick twitches as though he's answering for me, even while a metaphorical lightbulb illuminates above my head. I almost sob with relief to put words to what's bothering me. I feel a bit silly that I couldn't recognise sexual frustration for what it was. "Fuck. Yeah. Yeah, I think that's it."

Being around teenagers trying to have conversations about sex right under my nose must have triggered me subconsciously.

James shifts a little. *Squirms*, even.

Huh.

"How'd you know?" I ask him, and my heart speeds up with anticipation. I don't know why I'm suddenly anxious and excited to hear his answer, nor why my dick plumps up at my suspicions, either. "Are you—?"

"I haven't had sex in almost a year," he blurts out, and even in the darkness of the room, I can tell he's blushing. He gets this lilt to his voice any time he's embarrassed. It's a tell. "So, yeah, I'm pretty much perpetually horny. Especially when…" he stops himself. "Never mind."

"No." For some reason, I lower my voice, even though we're already speaking in hushed tones. I can feel blood rushing to my ears, aided by the increased beating of my heart. "Especially when what?"

He exhales, and I know he's about to admit something he's not proud of. "Especially when there's a warm body in my bed."

I'm a little confused at his embarrassment. "A warm bod—? *Oh*. Me?"

"Well, yeah, I guess. You're the first person I've shared a bed with in a long time."

"That makes sense," I shrug, as though hearing that sharing a bed with me makes him horny is no big deal. Because it's not. It's actually flattering. "Plus, we can't exactly go looking for hookups while we're pretending to be engaged, can we? Not locally, anyway. Knowing our luck, someone from the school will see us out and about or something."

Tension bleeds from his shoulders and I can feel the atmosphere in the room shifting as he relaxes. "Exactly," he says. "But, you know, we could take turns in the shower or something. Try and get some sleep after that."

Ugh. I've spent so much time alone with my right hand that I'm starting to think I'm engaged to it instead of my best friend.

Ding-ding-ding! The lightbulb in my brain flares back to life.

"Or," I start speaking, hoping he doesn't freak out because this idea is pretty damn genius, if I do say so myself, "we could help each other out."

His breathing hitches. "*What?!*"

"We're both horny, right?"

"Ev..."

"And we're both probably sick of the feeling of our own hands, right?"

"Evan..."

"And we love each other, right?"

"As best friends, Ev, not—"

"*Just* handies, Jay. Can we" —I lick my lips and give up trying to hide just how excited I am at the idea of having someone else touch my cock— "can we try it? Please? And if it's too weird, we can make one of those silence pacts, like the one we made when we were kids."

His breathing is laboured, and I can see the outline of his chest rising and falling rapidly. "I don't know..."

Brazenly, I shuffle closer and reach for his cock, and I'm not really surprised to find that he's just as hard inside his boxers as I am in mine. He cuts off his strangled protest and whimpers when I give him a tentative squeeze, assuming he likes being touched the same ways I do.

"Let me try, Jay," I whisper, stroking him through the satin. "It doesn't feel like you hate it."

"Fuck," he arches his hips. "O-okay. J-just tonight."

In my moment of relief and celebration, I stop thinking altogether and press my mouth over his in a joyful kiss. He stills, and I start to pull away, ready to apologise for taking this 'helping each other out' thing too far already, when his left hand cups the back of my head and presses my face back into his.

His tongue sneaks into my mouth and suddenly my accidental kiss turns into one of the most passionate kisses I've ever had in my life. It only gets better when his right hand snakes in between us and grasps my dick over the top of my boxers. He strokes me the same way I'm stroking him, without an ounce of hesitation, and it's *exactly* what I needed to feel all night.

"Fuck," he mutters against my lips when we pause the kissing to breathe, "Ev, fuck, this feels…"

"I know," I agree. "God, yes, Jay. Like that. Just…tighten up your grip a little. *Yes*. Just like that. *Ungh*, don't you dare stop."

"Can…can you…Ev…m-my balls…I…"

His plaintive begging is only making me hornier. Then his words register. "Yeah. Right. Pants off. Good idea."

We release each other reluctantly so we can shimmy out of our boxers, then we practically maul each other's mouths as we reconnect. "I-I've got lotion," he pants at our next pause for oxygen, "if that'll make this…easier."

"I could come just from this," I admit, surprised to hear how ragged and wrecked I sound just from having his hand on my dick and his tongue tangling with mine. "Your hand feels so good, baby."

"Oh, fuck," he arches his back, precum spilling from his head and down his shaft, and I grin as I reach lower to fondle his balls as a reward for the delightful reaction.

"You like that? When I call you baby?"

He whimpers. The non-verbal response probably means that he's embarrassed. He fucking shouldn't be.

"Fuck," I tell him, "Jay, that's so hot."

"I...I..."

Cutting off his stammering, I slam my mouth over his again, moaning as he tightens his grip on my cock and increases his speed. He's a quick study, my best friend.

"Jesus fuck," I wrench my mouth from his and nuzzle my bearded jaw against his cheek, pressing my lips up against his ear. "*Baby*," I croon, "just like that."

"*Ah!*" he shouts and arches his back as the warmth of his release coats my fist. I rush to cover his mouth with mine again, mindful that we need to stay quiet, and he moans and whimpers into the kiss while I milk him dry.

It's those whimpers that do me in and send me over the edge, coming all over his hand as I groan right back into his mouth.

I reluctantly end the kiss when my dick becomes too sensitive for his continued stroking, placing my sticky hand over his to stop his movement. Then I flop back onto my pillow, bringing my mess of our mixed fluids with me, and leaving Jay with some of his own as I dazedly murmur, "Holy fuck."

＊＊＊

We don't talk about it.

It's not for a lack of trying on my part, but we both crashed to sleep after cleaning up in the rudimentary ensuite attached to our room. Then we overslept our alarm and the morning was a mad rush of getting our shit together and then making sure the kids we were supposed to be in charge of were all lined up for the bus on time.

Obviously, we couldn't talk about it on the bus, nor could we talk about it on the drive back to James' place with Mia in the car.

And in the weeks since then, we just...haven't mentioned it.

So, we might not talk about it, but it's pretty much all I can think about.

I try in vain to remember every moment of it. How Jay's mouth tasted —minty and warm— how he smelled, the weight of his cock (thicker and longer than mine) in my hand. The sounds he made, the feeling of his dick swelling and then unloading over my fist...

I wonder if he was as moved by the experience as I was.

Because holy fuck: I made out with my best friend and exchanged a mutual handjob with him, and I fucking loved it!

I want to do it again.

...Can we do it again?

Like, okay, the night at camp was two best mates helping each other out. Bro jobs, or whatever. But, if we do it again, does it mean...more? Does it have to? Can't it just be an extension of the lie we're telling people? I mean, everyone involved with the school already thinks we're sleeping together. This just adds to the authenticity. That way, if Joey asks more questions about our relationship, we *won't* be lying. I'll feel much better about it if we're not.

"Earth to Evan," Jack waves a hand in front of my face, and he looks thoroughly amused when I blink back to reality, taking in the indoor soccer pitch and the team surrounding me. "Ah, you're with us again."

I cringe. "Sorry," I tell him, glancing at my watch. "I've got a bit on my mind."

"Yeah, well," Brett huffs and ties his long, dark hair up in his customary man bun, "try and concentrate on the game for the next sixty minutes, yeah?"

I salute him then, when his back is turned, turn the gesture into my raised middle finger.

Jack chuckles. "That's right," he says as I finish tying my boots, "you were hanging out with teenagers the last time we really chatted, weren't you?"

I snort. "I guess I've picked up some of their habits."

"That's okay," Connor teases as he pats his new son-in-law (who is a couple of years older than him) on the shoulder, "this one likes to channel his three-year-olds, too."

Jack rolls his eyes. "I'll teach them to call you Gramps, Con. You know I will."

I can't help but laugh at the scrunched, unimpressed expression on Connor's face as we all make our way onto the pitch.

Even though I mocked Brett earlier, I do manage to put all thoughts of Jay out of my head for the duration of the game. This one is fast paced, with the other team seeming to channel Brett's competitive energy. I spend the entire time focused solely on where the ball is and how to get it into the goal. I even manage to keep James from my thoughts during the half-time break, allowing myself to be distracted by the goings on the guys' lives.

Jack talks about his boys, acting a little strangely when Connor mentions his nanny, but otherwise seems to be well and truly settling into the single dad lifestyle. Brett asks Connor how wedded bliss is suiting him, and he laughs and admits that his and Will's relationship is very much the same as it was before they got married, but jokes that it's nice to be able to say that he has a sexy fireman husband (and brushes Jack aside when Jack reminds him that Will has retired).

"What about you?" Connor asks Brett. "Still single and loving it?"

Brett shrugs. "I miss having adult company sometimes," he admits. "Tom's going through a Spiderman phase and, while that means I get to watch a lot of Marvel movies, conversations at my place are pretty limited. And my work is kind of solitary."

I realise belatedly that I have no idea what it is he does for a living. I've always assumed, from the way he dresses and speaks, that he's a tradie of some sort. "Sorry," I apologise, "what is it you do again?"

"I'm a data architect for the uni up the road," he gestures vaguely southbound, but that could mean a couple of different universities. "It's a fancy title for someone who basically just collects, sorts and stores data. There's a bit of software development and management involved, too. I don't really need to talk to anyone much, and I'm pretty sure the faculty forget I exist."

I blink. I've got to learn to stop judging books by their covers. "Wow. That sounds...complicated." Pulling out my phone, I Google 'data architect' and then blink again at the average salary listed on SEEK. "Yeah. Yeah, wow. That's...more complicated than being an accountant, for sure."

He snorts. "Nah. I'd be a shit accountant." Checking his watch, he drops his water bottle to his feet and stands up again, shaking out his legs and shoulders. "C'mon, then. Let's win this thing."

Sadly, we do not win. We draw at two-all and basically collapse on the bench on the sidelines after the final whistle blows.

"That was a tight game," Brett says, grinning despite his exhaustion. "I'm buzzed now."

"I could sleep for, like, a week," Connor moans. "I don't know how the professionals do this."

"Speaking of," Brett says, "Did you hear they're starting up a professional team on the Coast now? It's probably still a year or so away from happening, but we could get season tickets for them instead of for the Roar in Brissie. Travelling up there every couple of weeks is a pain in the arse."

"That's assuming they're any good," Jack says, though I already know that he's on board. Jack's mad on almost all sporting events.

"It would be easier to bring the boys to games if we're travelling locally," I argue, just to further convince him.

His eyes light up. "True."

"I can bring Tom, too," Brett says. "Plus, I hear they're talking about bringing over someone from the UK Premier League to coach the Gold Coast team."

"Have we run out of Aussie coaches?" Henry, our goalie for the day and Connor's best friend, saunters over. He's a great guy, for a lawyer, but he only joins us every so often. He's got a toddler at home, and it sounds like he's super busy with his job, though, so none of us mind that he's in and out of the social games. It's not like we don't have lives on the side.

"Probs not, but it seems to be universally accepted that the Premier League is superior to the A-League," Brett is answering him. "I just hope they don't fill the team with newbies and ring-ins. It would be nice to have a solid local team."

Henry snorts. "Just so you don't have to travel up to Brissie?"

Brett laughs and nods. "Pretty much."

Connor, who has been typing away on his phone, scrunches up his nose. "Are they seriously trying to call the team The Thunder?" He looks up at us dubiously. "Don't they know that it sounds like the Thunder from Down Under? You know, the Vegas show with the male strippers?" He points a finger at Jack. "Don't you dare make a gay joke about me knowing about the strippers."

"I was only going to ask if you've been to Vegas," Jack tells him with faux innocence.

Henry, meanwhile, is frowning. "Isn't there a cricket team called the Gold Coast Thunder?"

Connor makes another face. "Who cares about cricket?" He yawns dramatically. *"Boring."*

I reach out to high-five him because, yeah: cricket is boring as fuck. As far as I'm concerned, it's a torture device, not a sport. Like, if I had any sort of super confidential information, that would be the way to get it out of me. In fact, I'd rather watch paint dry while having each of my toenails removed by force.

'No, no, please no. Don't make me watch cricket. I'll tell you anything you want!'

I fight the urge to snicker at my own internal thoughts.

At least they're not about James.

Ah, fuck it.

***

Strangely, the next time we see each other, things aren't awkward. I thought they might be, but James greets me the same way he always does, and conversation flows as easily as always, too.

Today's event for the school is simple tuckshop duty. We're assigned to assist with another couple. Like the school, the tuckshop is run with military precision. We each have our roles assigned to us for the day, with me serving at the window and

Jay packing orders, then all of us doing clean up and stocktaking, the couple of hours of mandatory volunteering are over relatively quickly.

James' phone pings as we make our way back through the school grounds and to his car. He reads the text, then looks at me. "Mia wants to sleepover at Rose's tonight."

"It's a Friday, so why not?" I ask with a shrug. "Sounds better than when she was dating whatshisname."

"Christian," he replies, distractedly, typing out a reply on his phone. "And they only went out three times before she enrolled here."

"And she hasn't gone out with anyone since?"

He shakes his head. "Nope. She *really* wants to get into NIDA, so everything's about getting noticed for her drama skills." He tucks his phone back into his pocket. "She says she has a change of clothes and a spare charger in her bag. I reckon they've been planning this all week."

"Give them a bit of credit," I laugh, stepping up to the passenger side of his car, "they would have come up with the plan last night. Otherwise, why wouldn't she just ask at the beginning of the week?"

"True," he acknowledges as we both climb into our seats. The doors close with muted thuds. "Well, my night just opened up. What are your plans?"

My stomach flips, flashbacks of the night at camp getting me all excited despite my best attempts to *not* make things weird or get my hopes up.

"I was gonna go home and go over some ledgers for work, but that's sounding less and less appealing."

The corner of his mouth twitches. "Pizza and beer at my place?"

I lean my head back and make an exaggerated drooling sound à la Homer Simpson. "You'd better not be fucking with me," I warn him. "You know pizza is my weakness." Carbs and cheese for life, and all that.

"I promise. I'll even buy."

Folding my hands over my chest, I mime swooning, "Be still my heart."

***

The pizza is, as expected, *just* what I needed. Delivered piping hot, the cheese is perfectly oozy, and there's an explosion of sauce and grease and deliciousness in my mouth on my first bite. I moan my enjoyment before James has even closed the door on the delivery guy.

"You sound indecent," he complains, but he's laughing as he steals the box from my hands and opens it to snatch his own slice of pepperoni-topped goodness.

"You'd know," I mutter around my mouthful without thinking.

He freezes with his drooping triangle of perfection held halfway to his mouth. His cheeks flame and he averts his gaze. "I thought we weren't talking about it."

Fuck.

I polish off my slice quickly, doing the 'ha ho ha ho' of having put something far too hot inside my mouth as I chew. Swallowing, I hold my hands in surrender. "Sorry," I tell him, "But...I *do* want to talk about it."

Closing his eyes, he seems resigned to his fate, even though he tries to protest with a weak, "Ev..."

"Wasn't it awesome for you? Because I haven't come that hard in...fuck, I can't even remember."

His blush deepens, running down his neck and beneath the collar of his shirt. It's adorable.

How have I never realised just how cute he is?

"You know it was," he mumbles and sets his unbitten slice of pizza back inside the cardboard box, shutting the lid to preserve the warmth. "But we also said—"

"I said if it was weird or bad we wouldn't talk about it. But it wasn't either of those things."

Finally, he brings his grey-green eyes up to meet mine. They flash with *something*. It's an undefinable emotion. "You don't think it's weird?"

"Why? Because we're two men who, until that happened, said we were both straight?"

I haven't really given much thought to what enjoying kissing and jerking off another man means for my sexual identity, because in the end I'm still me, but maybe James feels differently.

He rolls his eyes. "Because you've been my best friend since we were small."

Oh, I think.

"Oh," I say out loud. Then I frown. "Why would that make it weird? If anything, it proves the point about what we've been telling the school. We're just that comfortable with each other."

"I..." he starts to argue, then closes his mouth. "Well, I guess that's true."

"And it's only weird if we make it weird, right? Like...we can just be guys pretending to be in love and engaged, who get each other off behind closed doors. Nothing strange about that at all."

My best friend chuckles a little at that pronouncement. "Nothing strange about that?" he echoes with incredulity. "Really? *Nothing?*"

"We're best friends, Jay. This is the ultimate friends-with-benefits deal, isn't it? We've already acknowledged that we can't risk hooking up with anyone locally, and we both clearly need a bit of a release that *isn't* by our own hands, so…why not keep helping each other out while we're doing this fake engagement thing? And when it all ends, we'll still be mates, and we can go and date again."

"*Riiiight,*" he stretches the word out, arching one of his perfect, blond eyebrows. "It's that simple, is it?"

"Does it have to be complicated? I get off, you get off, we're all each other's got until we can call the engagement off. Hey," I grin, "that was almost poetic."

"Yeah, in the same way one times ten is *almost* one hundred."

The fact that he's cracking jokes is a good sign.

"So?" I prod in much the same way as I used to do when we were kids. "You in?"

He licks his lips, then nods almost imperceptibly. My whoop of victory is forestalled by his index finger being held up in front of my face. "We're going to need ground rules."

"Like?"

"Like not telling Mia. It'll confuse her."

"She's practically an adult," I argue, but then give it a little further thought. "But she might get the wrong impression, or ask questions we don't have answers to, so…okay."

"And it's just helping each other out. Nothing else about our friendship or our fake engagement changes."

"Well, duh. It's not like we need to take each other on dates or anything. You're already guaranteed entry into my pants." I waggle my eyebrows at him.

He rolls his eyes. "And there's no expectation of...penetration," he cringes as he says the word, and takes a sip of his beer, probably in a bid to cover his discomfort.

He is *so* not getting away with that.

"You've never had a girl play with your prostate while blowing you?"

He sputters and chokes on his beer, spraying his mouthful down the front of his shirt. "What the fuck, Ev?" he coughs out.

"It was a serious question. You don't need to be gay or even bi to enjoy anal." Tilting my head to the side, I ask, "You ever fucked a girl in the arse before?"

Making him blush is my new favourite pastime.

"*Ev...*"

"I have," I shrug. "Both things."

"Jesus Christ..."

"I'm just saying, it's not off the table if you wanna experiment with me."

"Y-you're saying—?"

"That you can play with my arse, yeah. No expectation for me to play with yours if you're not comfortable with that."

The amber liquid in James' bottle sloshes around as he shakily puts it down on the coffee table next to the pizza box. "That's...kind of intense, Ev."

"Nah. It'd probably be in a bed."

He blinks at me, then groans. "I'm being serious here!"

"So am I."

"You *just* cracked a really dodgy dad joke!"

"I'm a stepdad now, mate. I'm getting my practice in."

He gives a great big sigh and leans his head back, asking the ceiling, "How do I keep getting myself into these situations?"

The ceiling does not answer him. Or, if it does, I don't hear it.

Reaching for his beer again, he finally drops onto the couch seat next to mine, leaving half a seat's space between us. I take that as invitation to reopen the pizza box and I take another slice. It's not quite as good now that the cheese has had time to congeal, but it's still delicious.

After taking a couple of deep draws from the bottle, Jay asks, "Did...did you mention blow jobs before?"

"I did." As if to punctuate how okay I am with them, I lewdly suck sauce and grease from my index finger and then my thumb. James' cheeks turn a darker shade of pink, but his pupils dilate and he shifts in his seat.

He liked that.

"Do you..." his gaze drifts to my lips and his Adam's apple bobs. "I mean, is that, um, something you want to do? A-as part of this" —he waves his hand in the air between us— "arrangement?"

"I'm game for getting each other off in every possible way we can," I admit. "I mean, who better to try new things with than my best friend? We can laugh about it if it sucks or doesn't go the way we think it should, and we're comfortable enough with each other that we can ask questions or whatever as we go. It's a no judgement zone. It's just Ev and Jay having some fun."

For the first time since we started this conversation, he seems to relax. A slow smile tugs at his lips, bringing out the dimple in his left cheek. "That does sound nice," he says.

I nod and smile back at him, without a hint of playfulness. It feels like my expression is somehow both soft and serious when I tell him, "I mean it, Jay. You're my best friend. There's nobody else I'd trust with a friends-with-benefits deal like this."

"I wouldn't trust anyone else with this, either." James' confession is quiet and almost hesitant. He's always been the more cautious one of the pair of us. (The irony that he's the one who became a teen parent is not lost on me. Especially not now that we're "engaged" for Mia's sake. If there had been bets on it happening back then, both of us would have assumed it would be me.)

"So," a grin starts to spread across my face, "you're in? Friends with bennies?"

James being James, he just snorts and grabs his previously discarded piece of pizza. "Eat your dinner," he answers after finally swallowing his first bite, "and we'll see."

Chapter Nine

James

'We'll see' turns into me not protesting when Evan takes me by the hand and leads me into my own bedroom. Even though we're alone in the house, he closes and locks my bedroom door.

He knows me so well.

Something about having the door locked, even an in an empty house, helps to set me at ease. It feels more private, more *final*, and the fact that it was *him* making that choice without me having to say anything just reassures me that he wants this. He really wants this.

Whatever 'this' is.

Friends with benefits is what he called it. Best friends helping each other out so we don't accidentally ruin the whole 'fake relationship' scam we've got going.

Scam.

I don't like that word.

It feels wrong. We're not scamming anything out of anyone. Not really. I mean, yeah, we're not being entirely truthful, but I'm paying the insanely high tuition fees for Mia to attend the damn school. It's not like pretending to be in a same sex relationship has gotten us a free-ride or anything. I wouldn't have agreed to my daughter's crazy scheme if that had been the case. I have *some* morals.

"*Hey*," Ev's voice is low and soothing, and I lean into his touch as he rubs his palms over my biceps. "It's okay. There's no pressure here, Jay. If you want to back out—"

My hands fly up to grab his forearms, holding him in place in case he even thinks about pulling away. "No!" My cheeks burn at how loud my protest sounds in the silence of my darkened bedroom. "No," I repeat, quieter. "I...I'm on board." My hardening dick makes a valiant attempt to push his way out of my jeans, tenting the material but ultimately getting nowhere. I duck my chin, embarrassed by the fact that I'm already so hard, for the simple fact that we're in my bedroom together and that his hands are on me. "More than on board."

Ev lets go of my arms and, before I can lament the loss of his touch, grabs my hips, pulling me forward until my denim-clad erection is bumping against his. "Me too," he says, as if that wasn't obvious. "I haven't been able to stop thinking about that night at camp."

My breath catches and my traitorous cock twitches. "Me either."

I watch as his lust-blown gaze flickers to my lips, and my heart hammers. "Can I kiss you again?"

My tongue darts out, and I pretend to hesitate even though I've wanted little else than a repeat of *everything* that happened that night a few weeks ago. He seems to loom in closer and how have I never noticed that he's just that tiny bit taller than me?

Focus, James.

"Y-yeah," I breathe my answer when there's barely a sliver of space separating our mouths. "Please."

With how close he was, I'm surprised that the meeting of our lips is so tentative and gentle. I was expecting him to slam his mouth on mine, like he did in that uncomfortable bed, and press me up against the wall.

I think I might have liked that.

But I like this, too.

This careful, gentle touch of skin on skin. It feels reverent, somehow. Like he's taking his time memorising the feel and shape of my mouth. He hasn't even licked his tongue out against the seam of my lips yet, just...kissing me sweetly, breathing me in the same way I'm trying to do with him.

But...that can't be right. 'Friends with benefits' is just about shared orgasms, isn't it? Not *feelings*.

Maybe I'm over thinking this. Maybe he's just trying to get used to kissing a man without the haze of a rapidly impending orgasm fuelling his actions.

Not that mine isn't rapidly impending, mind you. It's kind of pathetic that I already feel like I'm teetering on the edge, with only the slow rub of his fully clothed bulge against my own, and a kiss so G-rated it could be televised to pre-schoolers.

Maybe if your erections are rubbing together it's not really that G-rated, a snide voice in my head sneers. *And it's probably creepy to think about pre-schoolers right now, too.*

What the ever-loving fuck is wrong with me?

All thoughts cease as Evan's hand cradles the back of my head, tilting me backwards as his tongue gently parts my lips.

Someone whimpers.

I have a sneaking suspicion it's me, especially when he makes a sexy as fuck growling sound and *then* the kiss fires up into the harder, more demanding one I was expecting from the start. A gasp is wrenched from my throat as I'm pushed against the door, fulfilling the fantasy I had only a few minutes ago, and Evan *grinds* into me, closing every single millimetre of space between our bodies.

At some point, Ev's lips leave mine, but my sound of complaint morphs into a moan as he mouths over my jawline, then —oh, my God— *nibbles* on my earlobe.

"You're so responsive," he whispers, and his voice sounds so husky and strained, I want to record the sound and replay it over and over. "*God,* Jay, you have no idea how hot you are, do you?"

I'm surprised my heart has enough blood to race as fast as it is, considering how painfully hard I am right now. "*Ev...*" I clutch at his arse, shamelessly rutting against him, wanting to beg but for what, I'm not sure.

"I don't think we'll even make it to your bed at this point," he continues in that far-too-seductive voice, moving his kisses along from the shell of my ear to my neck. He sucks lightly on my Adam's apple and —*Christ*— when did I throw my head back to give him the access? "I'm gonna jizz in my pants like we're fourteen again."

"Ev, I—" I start, then come to my senses, halting the confession that almost bubbled out of me in the heat of the moment.

Thankfully, the words that escaped me are innocuous enough that he just assumes I'm agreeing with him. Or on the cusp of pleading again. Or something.

The hand which was at my hip slides around and to the button of my jeans. "Can I—?" he asks.

I nod quickly. "*Yes.*"

Whatever disappointment I feel from the loss of his body against mine is replaced by nervous anticipation as he pops my button and unzips my fly. My cock takes full advantage of the movement, pushing out into the newly opened space, forcing the precum-dampened front of my boxer briefs to bulge obscenely out of my pants.

Then my heart skips at least three beats as Evan sinks to his knees on the carpet in front of me, tugging my jeans and underwear down to my thighs.

"*Holy fuck*," I breathe, looking down at him and the tableau he presents. My hand trembles as I reach for him, smoothing my palm over his hairless head. "Ev…" my voice comes out strangled and tight. I clear my throat. It doesn't help. "Y-you don't have to—"

"I want to," he's quick to cut me off, gazing up at me with a hunger that quite literally takes my breath away. "Let me, baby. Please?"

Baby.

I've never really been one for pet names. I rarely use them, and nobody has ever called me anything but my name.

Except for Ev.

And when he calls me baby, I can't quite describe the reaction it sets off inside me. It's like fireworks and butterflies all at once. It makes my heart squeeze and race at the same time. It makes my palms sweat and my cock twitch and dribble.

He's *very* aware of the latter. The dark pools of his irises shift from my face to my cock, and my skin burns from the intensity of his stare. When he looks back up at me again, repeating "Please?", I manage a tiny nod.

I watch with rapt attention as he slides his hands up my fuzzy thighs, bracing himself with one while taking the other to my throbbing erection. He wastes no time from there, grasping me with confidence and thumbing the sticky, weeping tip, gathering up a smear of precum before sliding his thumb between his pink, kiss-swollen lips.

When he hums, as though *pleased* by the taste, my brain short-circuits.

"*Fuck,*" I whimper, my balls drawing up tight when he smirks up at me, looking very smug and very satisfied.

"Soon," he winks. Then, before my brain can properly process what *that* means, his mouth closes around my weeping head and I moan loudly, the sound echoing through the stillness in my bedroom.

It's been an embarrassingly long time since I last received a blow job. Ev obviously isn't experienced in giving them, but the warm, wet suction and the twisting of his tongue feels so fucking good. Then there's the fact that it's *Evan* sucking me off, someone I love *(as a best friend, but still)* and that adds a whole new dimension which I've never really known before.

He grips the base of my cock and, using his spit for lube, squeezes and strokes what he can't take inside his mouth. The sounds he's making are like something out of a porno, all slurpy and messy and with the occasional gagging noise as he tries to take me further down his throat. In amongst all that, he's moaning and there's a distinctive *fap-fap-fap* sound underneath it all which, I realise, is him jerking himself off as he sucks me.

I don't know when he let go of my thigh, or when he unzipped his own jeans, and I don't care.

"*Oh my God,*" I moan and force my eyes open, also not quite sure as to when I shut them, and look down, trying to see *everything.* "E-Ev. Fuck. Ev. I don't...I'm close. But I don't...I don't want..." He opens his own eyes and stares up at me, my cock still moving in and out of those plump, wet lips. There's a sheen of moisture in his eyes, probably from all that gagging, and a delicious pink flush to his golden-coloured skin.

He's fucking gorgeous, I think, not stopping to consider just how very *not* 'friends with benefits'-like the thought is.

"*Ev*," I plead urgently, "I don't want to come yet. I don't—" The arsehole that he is, he hollows his cheeks and sucks harder, then *moans. "Nnngh."*

I grit my teeth and try to stave off the inevitable. When he lets go of my shaft and fondles my balls, it's all over. What little control I had evaporates and my orgasm thunders through me, forcing an incomprehensible shout from my lips as I erupt into his mouth.

I'm dimly aware of him *swallowing*.

"Jesus fuck," I mutter, slumping against the wall, my legs feeling like jelly while my heart practically bounces around my chest cavity like it's a ball in a pinball machine. I open bleary eyes to watch Ev lean back, still kneeling at my feet, jerking his cock in earnest.

That night at the camp, I didn't dare chance a look down at him, but now I take my fill. He's had my cock in his mouth, for fuck's sake, so it should be okay for me to look at his, right?

He's so hot, I think as I watch his hand shuttle up and down his length. His dick is what's probably considered an average size, but I've only got my own and porn to compare it to. Not that I care about his size. I've held it in my hand and jerked it to orgasm, and it felt absolutely perfect then, just like it felt perfect rubbing against mine through layers of cotton and denim.

It's darker than the rest of him, and an almost angry shade of purple at the head. I have the unexpected urge to know what it tastes like —what it feels like on my tongue— and I convince myself it's only because he just sucked mine until I came.

We've always been a little competitive, in a friendly way.

Still, I don't make a move to follow through on the random impulse, swallowing it back and watching as Ev pushes himself closer and closer to the edge. I can tell when he's getting close. His chest heaves and his breathing gets ragged and raspy. He's got a dark flush creeping into the collar of his shirt, and his eyes are turning glassy.

"Fuck," the awed murmur escapes me as his hips still, "Ev..."

It's on the tip of my tongue to tell him how unbelievably sexy his little show is, but the words fade away into a gasp as he groans and spills over his fist, rivulets of creamy liquid dripping over his flawless skin.

I lick my lips, my heart thumping almost as hard as if I just came again. "That was..."

His eyes are hooded as he slumps backwards, a lazy, pleased smile on his face. "Yeah," he agrees. "It was."

***

It keeps happening. Some nights, I tell Mia that I'm grabbing a beer with Ev and then we wind up exchanging hand jobs in his car, or we get each other off in his apartment. Others, when she's sleeping over a friend's place, he comes over to mine and we barely even make it to the bedroom.

I haven't ever had this much sex in my life, not even when I was at uni.

I feel like a teenager — constantly horny and ready to go at the drop of a hat, or zipper as it were.

And, as strange as it might sound, this whole friends with benefits thing seems to be making our friendship stronger. Ev and I hang out a lot more than we used to. We watch movies, talk about work, exchange orgasms, then fall into conversation about his indoor soccer team or plans for Mia's school holidays. It's effortless and fulfilling in ways I never imagined the arrangement could be.

Hell, if I could have a relationship like this, life would be perfect.

I mean a *real* relationship. Not a friendship with sex.

How is that different to a real relationship?

Thoughts like that one are dangerous and I push it aside, then attempt to bury it in the same place where I bury the rest of my 'Do Not Touch' memories.

"Penny for 'em?" Andi, one of my colleagues —the kind I consider a friend, though perhaps not a super close friend— asks as she drops down into the empty chair beside my desk. She spins around in it like a child, her red hair flying around her face with the motion. Her blue eyes sparkle at me as she prods, "Your thoughts. Penny for your thoughts?"

Understanding dawns over me as my brain sluggishly pulls out of the Evan-induced fog it has been in for weeks now. Months, even.

Years, if you'll be honest with yourself.

That thought gets buried, too.

"Just...thinking about Mia and her school stuff," I answer, and the lie comes so easily now that I wonder who I'm becoming.

Andi nods, her face lining with empathy. "They're really putting you through the ringer, huh? All that time you have to take off..."

"Thankfully, Collin is really good about letting me do that," I acknowledge.

"Yeah, well, you can do a lot of your job remotely," Andi shrugs. "We all can. Why they insist on making us work in this office is beyond me. Well," her tone turns a little snide, "aside from justifying the overpriced lease. I reckon commercial industries could topple the real estate market, given half a chance."

"It's one big conspiracy theory," I agree placatingly, nodding my head. "I know."

The thing is, she's not wrong. I can do the bulk of my job from anywhere. I'm in marketing, and I can plan campaigns and analyse data without being in the office. We can even hold virtual meetings with clients and potential clients — something we do have to do more often than not, given that a lot of our clients are based interstate or overseas nowadays.

Nevertheless, I quite enjoy my job, and I consider myself lucky to have a boss who is happy to be as flexible with my hours as he is. I'm not going to rock the boat and complain about company policy when he can't do much to change it, either. Andi has no such qualms.

"Anyway," I cut her off before she can really get going on her usual rant, "It's been, what, six months? Only another eighteen to go and then Mia will be graduating."

"Less than eighteen months," Andi nods. "Especially when you count school holidays."

"Shit," I look at the calendar, "June holidays are coming up soon."

"Mia's sixteen, she can fend for herself at home for a couple of weeks," Andi waves my panic aside, her pink nail polish glittering in the light from the fluorescent bulbs above our heads. "It's not like she's a little kid who needs to be enrolled in vacation care."

"I know, but I was hoping to spend some of the holidays with her," I admit, feeling a bit crestfallen that, with all the time I've had to take off to deal with the school's demands, I completely forgot to organise some actual time off work. "She already prefers hanging out with her friends over me. Once she graduates and is officially an adult…" I trail off, upset at how fast my kid is growing up.

Andi leans over and rubs my bicep. "There's always the Chrissie hols."

In another six months, and far harder to get time off because every man and his dog want time off over Christmas. Still, I nod. "And September, too."

"That's the spirit," she cheers, oblivious to the flatness in my tone.

I whip my phone from my pocket to make a note to investigate the dates and blink at the text notification from Ev and about a hundred (okay, *four*) missed calls from the school. My heartrate increases as I wonder what's gone wrong.

"What's up?" Andi leans over, craning her neck to peer at my phone screen.

Furrowing my brow, I tilt it away from her view. I don't need her seeing anything racy from Ev and getting the wrong idea.

What, asks the voice in my head with droll amusement, *like the silly idea that you're fucking your best mate?*

I ignore my inner monologue in preference of reading Ev's text.

Ev:

> *Mia's sick. Picking her up cos school called me. Couldn't get a hold of you.*

"Damn it," I hiss, rapidly typing my response that I'll meet him at my place before ramming my phone in my pocket. "Mia's sick," I explain as I shut my laptop and start gathering my things. "Ev's picked her up, but I'll tell Col that I'm working from home this afternoon."

Andi's expression droops, but then morphs into one of sympathy. "Poor thing," she coos, pouting up at me once my laptop bag is packed and I'm pushing to my feet. "Hopefully it's just a twenty-four-hour bug."

I nod, grimacing. "I suppose that's one benefit to having an almost-adult kid. I don't need to chase her around the house with a vomit bucket and a towel."

Scrunching her nose, Andi shakes her head. "I'm kind of glad I don't have kids yet."

"They're not for the faint of heart." I pat down my pockets, checking for my phone, wallet, and keys.

Andi sighs and gets up, out of the seat at the spare desk. She gives me a lop-sided smile. "Maybe I need to find a guy who has already done all the hard work for me, and then I can be a cool stepmum to a nice, easy, independent teenager."

I chuckle, thinking about how much work it has been chaperoning other peoples' teens, and I shake my head. "Teenagers are harder work than toddlers, I reckon." I crane my neck around her, attempting to peer into Collin's office. His door is open and, thankfully, he's at his desk. "I've gotta run," I say, easing around her and heading in my boss's direction. Over my shoulder, I add, " I'll be logged into Teams in about an hour."

Andi lets out what sounds like a frustrated sigh, but I can't help that my kid is sick. Even though Ev is perfectly capable of keeping an eye on her for a few hours, she's still my responsibility and I want to make sure she's okay.

Chapter Ten

Evan

"**Y**ou sure you don't want me to take you to the GP?" I ask the miserable teenager beside me. She's curled up under a soft, grey-coloured throw blanket, clutching a plastic bowl to her chest as though she might hurl again at any second.

Her skin is pale and clammy, and her eyes are red rimmed from the tears she shed during her last bout of violent vomiting over the toilet.

Mia shakes her head. "No." She closes her eyes and swallows convulsively. "I just wanna rest."

"I'm going to get you some ginger ale or lemonade or something," I insist, trying to think of what else my mum used to do for me when I got struck down with gastro. "Maybe some dry crackers or something, too."

Mia gags and holds the bowl tighter. "I can't even keep water down right now."

I have to admit, getting the 'your kid is sick' call from her school was kind of surreal. In all the years I've been her Godfather and Jay's emergency backup, I've never once been called into action. I can only assume that Jay was in a meeting, or away from his phone, and I was more than happy to step in in his stead.

It was an eye-opening experience.

Firstly because I blindsided my boss with having to pack up and leave work suddenly, getting the side-eye from colleagues who know I don't have any children of my own. Then driving across the Gold Coast to her school, feeling worry churn my stomach.

What if there was something actually wrong with her; something more insidious than a stomach bug? What if she threw up again while she was waiting for me to come and get her? What if she was disappointed that it was me picking her up and not her dad?

Then seeing her in the school's office, looking impossibly young and sad and sickly, gave a tug to paternal instincts I never knew I had. I felt helpless, knowing that there's nothing I can actually do to make her feel better. She has to ride out the bug by herself.

Has Jay felt like this every single time he's had to collect her from sick bay all these years?

"You need to keep hydrated," I insist, but she whines at the back of her throat and it stops me from getting up from my spot on the couch beside her. Instead, I open my arms, "Come cuddle?"

"I don't want you to get sick, too."

I shrug. "I've got plenty of sick leave up my sleeves. It's a risk I'm willing to take."

Despite being sixteen, Mia doesn't need any more convincing. She shuffles over, leaning her head against my chest, still huddled under her blanket with her bowl held to her chest like a favoured teddy bear.

I stroke her soft, blonde hair —which is a little greasy at the moment, likely from her sweating and illness— and try to ignore the squeezing of my heart at how domestic this feels.

I've always been the fun 'Uncle', for lack of a better term. Aside from when she was small and I needed to stand in solidarity with James against her temper tantrums, I've never really had to do anything quite so...*paternal* with Mia. I don't think I ever even changed a nappy when she was a tot. She's been my best little bud, a partner in crime (pranks) against her dad, and a kid I've loved but have only really ever experienced the 'fun side' of.

But this? This feels more intense, somehow. More serious. It hits me just how much James has had on his shoulders over the years, but also how much trust he has in me as his backup emergency contact.

I try not to dwell too much on the emotions that realisation stirs up.

We're best friends and have been since we were nine. Of course Jay trusts me. It doesn't need to mean anything more than that.

It *can't* mean anything more than that.

Can it?

***

"Hey," Jay shakes me awake gently, and it takes me half a moment to get my bearings.

I must have fallen asleep on his couch with Mia cocooned against my side. My arm is draped around her, holding her close, like I've seen James do countless times over the years. The rim of her plastic bowl is digging into my stomach, but I don't dare move it or her.

"Hmm?" I hum as I try to rouse myself from a half-wakeful state. James' face comes into focus in front of me. He's crouching down, his grey-green eyes lined with concern.

"How is she?" he asks, keeping his voice so low it's barely audible.

"*Wha'timezit?*" I ask by way of reply. He holds up his phone, the lockscreen showing a photo of the three of us taken at the musical in Brisbane a few months ago. My heart gives a tug at the wide grins on our faces.

We look like a real family…

Focus, Evan.

The clock says it's just gone noon. I picked Mia up around ten. I can't believe I fell asleep on the couch with her. "She's been asleep about an hour," I tell him, my voice gravelly from my nap. I glance at the empty bowl sandwiched between our bodies. "Hasn't been sick again."

My stomach does a funny little flip at the emotions that flicker in his gaze as he turns his attention to Mia. "Hopefully the sleep'll help chase off the bug," he muses softly. Then he looks back at me with gratitude and chagrin. "Thanks for getting her. I missed the calls. We had an early morning meeting and I totally forgot to take my phone off silent."

"Don't mention it," I brush off his thanks. "I never get to do the 'dad to the rescue' thing. It gave me a better appreciation for how you must've felt for all these years."

"I hate that she's sick, but I do enjoy the cuddles," he admits, reaching out to carefully brush some of Mia's blonde locks back behind her ear. "It takes me back to when she was little."

"She's always been a sweet kid. Makes me wonder if I shouldn't have settled down, had one of my own."

I don't know where that confession comes from, but it doesn't sit right with me. Not entirely. Thinking back over the women I've dated, none of them would have worked for that particular fantasy, and not only because we obviously broke up. None of them gave me any warm, fuzzy, settling down feelings.

But sitting here with Mia and Jay does.

I shift uncomfortably as that thought crosses my mind. I'm starting to come to a conclusion about my feelings for my best friend, and it's confusing as all hell.

I can't deny that I feel some sort of attraction to him. The fact that I've had his cock in my mouth and have enjoyed it each and every time is probably a sign that I'm not as straight as I believed I was. And I've said time and time again that I love him, because he's been my best friend since we were nine...

But the 'benefits' part of our arrangement has started to feel like *more* than just sexual release. It's putting thoughts in my head that I never expected to think, and making me want things I never thought I would want.

Like settling down.

Like having a family.

Like...being with James. As in *being* with James. In every possible way.

Why can't I make these feelings stop?

It's not that I'm ashamed of them, or afraid of what they say about my sexual identity. It's more that I'm afraid of the damage they can do to my closest friendship. It's also that I don't entirely trust that they're real.

What if I'm only feeling this way because of all the forced proximity between us? Because of the shared orgasms and our history as best mates? What if I were to tell Jay how I feel…only to realise that I was wrong, and that the love I feel for him really is platonic? There wouldn't be any going back from that.

But what if I don't say anything and miss a chance to see where this thing between us could go? Assuming it could go anywhere at all…

Ugh.

I really need to talk to someone about this. Someone who isn't my best friend. Even that thought seems kind of confusing because, if this was happening with anyone else, Jay would be the first person I'd reach out to to help me sort out my thoughts. It's just that he's the centre of them, and I need an unbiased perspective.

"You know you're only thirty-five, right?" Jay's reply to my random admission brings me right back into the moment. He moves his hand from toying with his daughter's hair, to squeezing my knee. The simple action sets all of my convoluted thoughts tumbling about again, but he keeps on taking, oblivious to my inner turmoil. "Like…most guys our age are only just starting to settle down. You still have heaps of time."

"Yeah," I acknowledge, "you're right."

It's not like I can say anything else to him. At least, not right now. Not until I know for sure what —if anything— to say to him.

***

Between commitments at the school, catching up on my work, and generally stressing out about the fact that I'm pretty sure I'm falling in love with my best mate, I miss a couple of our social soccer games. Finally being able to return to the indoor pitch is a relief, like a sliver of normalcy in a life I feel is unravelling at my feet.

I'm buoyed by the prospect of being able to shed my frustrations on the soccer pitch again. To run, and kick a ball, and lose myself in the game. And, when I've got my boots on and I've stretched out my out-of-practice muscles, I spy Jack's large, tattooed form slumped on the bench, with one boot on and the other dangling from his hand as he stares unseeingly in front of him.

"Earth to Jack," I ruffle his hair, and he gives himself a shake before he glares up at me. I return his glare with a grin. "You with us, mate?"

He rolls his eyes, but hurries to get his second boot done up. "Shut up. I was lost in thought."

"Yeah, we noticed," I wave my hand vaguely at the rest of the team waiting on the pitch. "Game starts in three. You up for it?"

"Of course I am."

Something in his tone gives me pause. I can resonate with it. Letting go of my teasing, I ask, "You wanna talk about it?"

Jack's a bit defensive, though. He arches an eyebrow and cocks his head. "You wanna talk about whatever's been keeping you from the past few games?"

Uh, nope.

"It's complicated."

"Yeah, well, welcome to my life." He's usually a pretty happy-go-lucky guy, so I just watch as he gets to his feet and runs through a couple of on-the-spot warm-ups to limber up for the game.

I don't know why, but I blurt, "I think I'd be better off talking to Connor about my issues. No offense or anything."

"Why Con?" He asks, and then, while I'm scrambling to *not* accidentally out myself when I'm not even sure how I identify, he carries on with a shrug. "You know what? It's not my place to ask. You've got his number, right?"

I just nod, still not sure what to say or how to say it.

"Cool," Jack says. "He's a good guy and a great listener. I...actually need his advice, too."

That takes me by surprise, but then I want to facepalm. There's no way Jack would be going through some sort of sexual identity crisis. "Oh, because of the kids? I figured you'd ask your dad any parenting type questions, not your stepdad." I can't help sneaking in that last little tease. Banter's what we do, after all. Deep and meaningfuls with my soccer mates just feel weird.

Even if I do want to have a deep and meaningful conversation with Connor.

"Stop calling him that," Jack complains. "Even if you're technically right, it's weird."

"Oi!" Brett calls from the pitch. "Are you ladies planning on joining us?"

"You wish we were ladies," Jack sasses him as we head over to take our places on the pitch, "have you seen how freaking aggressive the women's league is? We'd kick major ass if we played like them."

"I'll kick your arse if you're not careful," Brett tells him, then points his finger accusingly. "Try not to let the ball near the goal this game."

They toss a couple more barbs each other's way, and then the game kicks off. It's rough for a friendly social match. The other team is even more competitive than Brett, and there are yellow cards thrown around by the ref within minutes.

It's fast-paced, brutal and exhausting, and it proves the perfect distraction from my personal woes. Brett manages to kick the winning goal with five minutes left of play and, while the other team complain to the ref about offside rules, the poor volunteer counts the goal and I'm surprised there isn't a riot in place of the final few minutes. Once the whistle blows, we shake hands and fist bump the other guys, but it's pretty obvious they're not happy, muttering under their breaths about unfair advantage and shit.

I wander back to the bench with Brett, ruffling his short hair and celebrating his winning goal raucously. I haven't felt this light in ages, and I'm going to ride the high for as long as possible.

I keep joking with Brett as we start packing up our stuff, taking off boots and replacing them with sneakers, then shoving the lot into our sports bags. I'm keeping half an ear on Connor and Jack's conversation, wanting to catch the former so I can hopefully borrow him for a private chat.

I know I'm probably stereotyping in my assumption that the only out gay man I'm friends with is my best option for such a conversation, but Connor is a good guy. He's open, honest, and down-to-earth. He's also married to a man and, seeing as I'm confused about wanting to do the same, I feel like he's the best person to talk to about that.

Then Jack derails my plans entirely with his own admission that he slept with his Manny.

Jack.

Big, brawny, tattooed fireman Jack —a guy with a reputation as being a ladies man and a bit of a playboy to boot— slept with his *male* nanny.

My heart hammers as he sums up his story, not seeming at all fazed that he just came out as bi to his indoor soccer team…not that any of us care — in fact, Brett even congratulates him and claps him on the back. I file that reaction away in the back of my mind to mull over in private.

Even though our situations are nowhere near the same, I hang on Jack's every word and hold my breath for Connor's advice as I follow them toward the exit.

I listen intently, unable to stop myself from double checking when Connor suggests that Jack talks to Leo (his kids' nanny). I feel my cheeks heat when Jack arches his eyebrows at me, but then Connor starts in on his assumptions about Leo and why he asked Jack for space after things between them got intense, and I'm all ears again.

"He's also a guy whose life experiences to date have shown him that it's easier to be the one to cut ties and control his own heartache." We exit the building and my sweaty, heated skin cools in the evening breeze. Our shoes crunch on the gravel as I continue to follow them across the carpark, and Connor keeps talking, "I know you didn't experience the sort of rejection that he has, but you didn't date beyond casual hookups for a reason, Jack."

Jack stops for a moment, clearly dumbstruck. "How'd you…"

Connor rolls his eyes. "Really? Because I don't think commitment-phobes are afraid of the companionship or the sex on tap. I reckon they're afraid of not having control of their feelings. They're afraid of having their hearts hurt."

"To be fair," Brett adds, also following along, even though his car is parked in the opposite direction, "some people avoid commitment because they have FOMO and they feel like 'settling'," he emphasises the word with finger quotes, "means they're missing out on God only knows what opportunities, or that they're choosing the wrong person or whatever." The derision and bitterness in his tone is out of character for him. "Relationships are mundane to them. Or they're against the idea of any kind of responsibility and losing their independence."

Connor nods and leans against the side of his SUV. "Yeah, well, do you think Jack's like that?"

After Brett and I shake our heads, he nods again, his lips pulling up a little smugly. "Neither do I. So, that leaves my hypothesis...which was right, by the way." He looks over at Jack. "Wasn't it?"

As Jack agrees with him, I feel completely vindicated that Connor is the right choice to talk to about my issues. He's pretty wise for a guy our age. I soak in every word he speaks to Jack, suddenly feeling less confused about my own feelings. Jack's situation is more complicated than mine, really.

He's still getting to know Leo, whereas I know James inside and out. We have a solid history, and we've never had an issue communicating...until now. And that's my fault. I need to trust in that history. I need to trust that, if...no, *when* I tell him that I want our fake relationship (which doesn't feel fake) to become a real one, that he won't laugh at me or destroy twenty-five years of friendship over my sudden revelation. Even if he turns me down, or tells me that he doesn't reciprocate my feelings, I need to trust that he'll still be my best mate. Yeah, things might be awkward for a while, but he's a good guy. It's part of what I love about him.

So, like Jack and Leo, I need to suck it up and communicate properly. That seems like common sense, the more I think about it.

Look at me being a grown up.

When Connor makes a crack about his age gap with Will being bigger than Jack and Leo's, the weight on my shoulders has been removed, and I can't help but teasingly ask, "Are we playing 'yours is bigger than mine' now?"

Connor waggles his eyebrows back at me, almost leering. "Don't start a competition you'll lose, man."

It's hard to pretend to be scandalised when all I want to do is laugh. Jack redirects the conversation again, and I —having received the advice I was searching for, even if via conversational osmosis— make plans to go and talk to my best friend.

Chapter Eleven

James

"**W**hat are you doing here?" I ask as Ev sneaks into my bedroom, closing the door behind him with a quiet *snick.*

My cheeks flame in the semi-darkness of my room, lit only by the lamp on my bedside table, because if he had been even five minutes later, he would have caught me with my hand down my pants. As it is, I quickly snap the lid of my laptop shut, not wanting him to see the porn I was loading up.

The *gay* porn.

That's a revelation I've been trying to avoid: the fact that I seriously do get off thinking about other men. But ever since Ev and I started helping each other out, it's all I've been able to think about.

"I..." Ev steps towards the bed, then hesitates, biting his lip.

It's not often that I see him anything but confident, so it has me sitting up straighter against the headboard. "Ev?"

"I wanted to talk to you..." he says, and something in his tone makes the hair on the back of my neck stand up straighter. "It...it couldn't wait. I…" Scrubbing his palm over his face, he mutters, "Fuck. I'm making a mess of this already."

"Evan," I say his name in the same tone I usually use when Mia's pushing boundaries. It seems to startle my best friend out of his head and his attention snaps to my face, his gorgeous dark eyes wide with surprise. I pat the space beside me. God knows he should feel comfortable in my bed by now. "Sit. Tell me what's wrong."

He eyes the space beside me warily and my heart squeezes.

Has he worked it out? That I have feelings for him, I mean. That I've broken the rules of our friends-with-benefits arrangement? That I've gone and made things between us weird?

When he steels himself and sits, I shove my discarded laptop off the bed entirely. It crashes to the carpet with a dull *thud*, but all of my attention is on Evan.

"What's wrong?" I repeat, this time more softly. Cautiously. Because I'm terrified of his answer.

"We're…um," he starts, then stops and takes a long, calming breath. In…and out. He clears his throat, then looks me in the eye. His expression is surprisingly serious and unreadable.

My heart plummets to my stomach.

He knows.

I open my mouth to speak, but I have *no* idea what to say.

He takes the decision for me.

"We're not fake dating," he says firmly. "Or fake engaged."

"W-what?"

"We're not…" he licks his lips. "Jay. We're *actually* dating."

That…is not at all what I thought he was going to say.

I blink. "Uh…?"

"We go out to dinner. Or have dinner here. We share our thoughts about our days, our jobs, the shows and movies we wanna watch…"

"Yeah, but we've always—"

He holds up his index finger and places it over my lips. "I'm not done, baby."

Baby.

My brain short-circuits.

Oblivious, Ev keeps talking, "My point is, we go on dates. We kiss. We have sex. Jay, we're dating. For real. And," he swallows roughly, Adam's apple bobbing as he reaches for my hand. My left hand. He thumbs over the tacky fake engagement ring I haven't yet taken off for the night. "I…don't feel like this is fake, either. I mean, the ring is, and maybe we can fix that one day, but…what it stands for. The promise of forever. I…I feel like that's real, too."

Holy shit, I think to myself, the reality of his words hitting me in the chest.

I think of the months we've spent pretending to be a couple. I think about how effortless that has felt. How holding his hand and kissing him for show hasn't really felt like it was for show at all.

I've enjoyed it.

Then there's the fact that it spilled over into our private lives. That we've been going out on dates under the guise of best friends just hanging out. Only best friends don't come home afterwards to exchange hand jobs, do they?

"Oh my God," I exhale, certain that shock is written all over my face as the truth of it all sinks in. "We're dating."

Ev nods, still stroking his thumb over my gaudy ring, and he lets out a breathy, nervous-sounding laugh. "Are you…okay with that?"

"Are you? Because…I thought you were straight."

Ev snorts. "I'm pretty sure straight men don't feel the way I do about kissing other guys. Even when it's their best mate."

The feelings I've kept buried since we were fourteen start to dig their way out of their too-shallow graves. Then again, I was *just* watching gay porn: who the hell am I trying to kid?

I can feel my heart beating rapidly, as afraid of labelling myself now as I was as a teenager. "Oh."

As if he can read my mind, Evan hurries to add, "But I'm not telling you how to feel or how to identify yourself. I'm just saying that for me...I might be realising a few things."

I bite my lip. He reaches out and gently tugs it free with his thumb, and I freeze when he does. He carefully retracts his hand and offers me a lopsided smile. It makes my stomach flutter.

"Yeah," he muses, "I'm...not straight. Maybe bi? Maybe pan? I don't really care about the label at this point."

"You don't?"

"Nope," he shakes his head. "Nothing about me is any different with a label." That damned smile is back. "I'm still the same Evan I've always been, just with a bit more self-awareness."

It takes me a moment before I quietly confess, "You've always been braver than me."

He brings a hand up to cup my cheek and my eyes flutter closed as he speaks. "You don't have to label yourself. We don't have to put a label on this...and, yeah, I know I just have by saying we're really dating, but we can just—"

"I've had a crush on you since we were fourteen." My heart is somehow torn between hammering inside my ribcage and squeezing itself to death. Is this a heart attack? It feels like it might be.

"What?"

"I...that night. The one we don't talk about. I..." Fuck, I can't do it. It's somehow even more humiliating to admit it now than it was back then.

"Hey, hey, hey," Ev's voice is soothing as he pulls me in for a hug. I go willingly, resting my head on his shoulder while his big, warm palm strokes my back. "It's just me. I'm never gonna judge you, Jay."

"I..." It should be easier to do this without looking at him. I breathe in the scent of his cologne, faded but embedded in the fibres of his white cotton t-shirt, and I take a deep breath. "You were having a wet dream...all moaning and stuff...and I...I was awake and I..."

"Jerked off watching me?" he asks calmly, without a hint of amusement or censure. His voice is a low rumble through his chest, vibrating against mine, and I nod, unable to speak past the lump which has suddenly formed in my throat.

"*Baby*," he repeats the endearment that he has only ever used during our moments of 'helping each other out'. "James" —my breathing hitches because we never really use our full names, either, and, oddly, I *like* the way he says it— "we were fourteen. A stiff breeze would have me jerking off sometimes." We both chuckle, then his voice softens as he asks, "Why didn't you say anything? About your crush?"

"You kept talking about Sasha McNaught's tits, for one thing," I answer, cringing when what was supposed to be a playful retort comes out bitter to my own ears. He must hear it, too, because he rubs my back a little bit harder, and I forge on, "And I was...confused, I guess. I liked girls, too, and I thought—I thought it was just a weird hormonal thing and it would go away. And

I thought it did…until we started this whole fake relationship thing.”

“Which isn't really fake anymore.”

“Was it ever?”

“I mean,” he snorts lightly, “we both thought it was. It's hard to draw a line, though, when we were already so close. But, I mean it: we don't need to label ourselves or whatever this is between us.”

“I'm pretty sure I'm bi,” I mumble into his shoulder, feeling an elated sort of fluttering in my chest at how much easier that was to say than I assumed it would be. Maybe his bravery and confidence has rubbed off on me? Maybe just knowing that I'm not alone in this is enough for me to be brave, too? “And I want to call you my…boyfriend? Partner?”

“Best mate. Fiancé. Lover. All of the above.”

I screw my nose up and pull back. “Lover? Really?”

He waggles his eyebrows and coos, “What about paramour? Flame? Love muffin?”

It's impossible to keep a straight face. I slap a hand over my mouth to contain the bark of laughter that just attempted to escape. “Stop it,” I hiss at him. “Mia's home.”

Even though the seriousness of our conversation has passed, his jovial mood shifts back into a softer one. “How is she?”

“Better. Back at school…until Friday, anyway. Then it's school holidays for two weeks.”

“You want me to take some time off to hang out with her? I've got heaps of leave…what?”

I'm sure I'm the human personification of the heart-eyed emoji right now. “I love you,” I tell him, as if my face isn't giving all my thoughts away. I grasp the back of his neck and tug him towards me, crushing my lips to his in a kiss that has been building up for over twenty years.

There's no guilt this time. No fear. No worries that he will find out my sad, sordid secret feelings for him. Because they're *not* sad, or sordid, or even a secret anymore.

I kiss him with every ounce of elation and liberation I feel. For the first time ever, I am being completely honest with myself and with him. The fact that he reciprocates my long-held feelings is almost unbelievable.

His fingers in my hair and the gentle way he's pushing me onto my back are so real, though. His breath, turning ragged and needy against my lips, is real. The scratch of his beard against my day's growth of stubble is real. And his erection rubbing up next to mine is *very* fucking real.

"Can you be quiet?" I ask him when he groans and ruts against me. "Because if you can't, we're gonna have to stop for now."

"Fuck," he mutters, still rocking his hips, "we're not stopping...but I need you naked."

I prop up on my elbows. "Naked?" In all the weeks we've been pretending to be best friends with benefits, we've stayed dressed in one way or another. Cocks have been exposed, jerked off, rubbed against each other and sucked, but we've never been completely without clothes.

I can't help feeling like a virginal teenager again, suddenly unsure of my dad bod next to his athletic one.

Ev sits back up on his knees between my spread legs, resting his butt on his heels while he strokes his hands over my thighs and calves. "Jay...baby, you know I've seen you naked a million times."

"Yeah, but..."

I wasn't trying to turn him on then. That was just guys getting changed after gym sessions, or beach days, or that one ill-fated game of squash he made me play. *This* is different.

"The only butt I want to hear about is yours. Or—no." He smirks. "Mine. When you fuck it."

"Jesus Christ, Ev."

"Not tonight," he adds, probably able to read my trepidation at having *that* sprung on me on top of everything else tonight. "I'd want time to prepare. Clean house properly and stuff, y'know? And...I love Mimi, but..."

"I get it. I'd rather have the house to ourselves, too. At least for the first time. Assuming you like it enough for other times." My eyes widen as another thought hits me, adding to my fear that he won't find my body sexy enough. "What if I'm bad at it? What if...Ev, what if we don't like it?"

"Then we don't like it," he shrugs.

"But..." my throat tightens up with mounting panic and, despite my best efforts, I sound like I'm on the verge of tears when I continue, "how could we stay together if we don't like the sex?"

"Anal isn't the only way to have sex."

"But—"

"Have you enjoyed the bjs? The handies? Rubbing off against each other?"

I nod, my cheeks burning. "But...I haven't...y'know..."

"If you can't talk about sex, Jay, you shouldn't be having it," he teases, using the same line I've been throwing at Mia since I gave her The Talk.

I take the bait, rolling my eyes. "Blown you. I haven't blown you." I hesitate before asking, "What happens if I suck?"

"That's kind of the idea."

"*Ugh.* Evan. I'm being serious."

He sniggers. "I know. And it's adorable."

"I swear to God, you can get out of my house if you're just going to mock me."

"Baby, have you *ever* had a blow job you hated? Like, even your first one? When Michelle Parker used her teeth?"

I wince at the memory. I'd still come all over her face —accidentally— when I was pulling away from those very same teeth. So sue me, the wet suction of her mouth was still pretty damn amazing and...*oh.*

"You'll be fine," Ev nods, as if reading my mind. "And if you hate giving head, that's okay, too. We can buy toys and find what works and what doesn't."

"And you'd be okay with that?" I can't help double checking. "A life without getting head? A life without fucking someone? A life without *being* fucked."

"Yep," he nods, then grins. "*Toys*, James. Toys, and lube, and coming in every other way with the man I love." His expression slackens with surprise, and he blushes a little. "Huh. I've never said it out loud before. Not like that." He cocks his head. "I love a man. *Wow.*"

"Is reality kicking in now? You finally going to have a panic attack-slash-identity crisis? Because I've been having one for twenty-odd years."

Laughing softly, he shakes his head. "Yeah, nah," he answers. "Just...kinda' hit me. Putting it like that. Hearing myself say it." Then he leers. "And you're still not naked."

I roll my eyes, but move to sit up so I can tug my shirt over my head. I'm just about to chuck it on the floor when there's a knock at my door, causing both me and Ev to freeze.

"Mia?" I ask, as if it could possibly be anyone else.

"Yeah," her voice is tentative on the other side. "Um. Are you...uh...I thought I heard voices."

I lock eyes with my best friend (my...boyfriend?) and see my thoughts mirrored on his face.

Shit.

Chapter Twelve

Evan

This is not how I imagined telling Mia that our fake relationship isn't quite so fake anymore...if it ever was to even start with. I don't think James is ready yet, either, and I smooth my hands over every part of him that I can reach, trying to calm him down. I press my index finger to my lips, conveying that I can be quiet, and then I slide my phone from my hip pocket and waggle it between us.

"You're on the phone," I mouth.

His kiss-swollen lips part into a perfect 'O' shape. I suspect my plan to *finally* feel them wrapped around my dick has been foiled by his kid. Who knew sixteen-year-olds were such cockblockers?

He clears his throat and raises his voice towards the door, answering, "Yeah, uh, I'm on the phone. To Ev."

"Oh," her voice is slightly muffled. "Okay." There's no shuffling or stomping of feet to indicate that she's walking away yet. A moment later, she says, "It's a bit late, isn't it?"

I glance down at my phone screen. It's only ten. We're not geriatrics.

"We're not in our seventies yet," Jay calls back with a laugh, and it makes me smile because *how* are we so in sync with each other? "But it's definitely your curfew."

There's a temperamental teenaged "*Ugh*" from the other side of the door, before Mia says, "Fine." Then, less moody, she adds, "Night, Dad. Love you."

Aww. My heart goes all gooey for a moment.

"Night, Mimi," Jay calls after her. "Love you, too."

With the sexy vibes well and truly dissipated, I collapse onto the mattress beside James and tug him against me for a cuddle. I press my lips to his blonde head and allow tonight's events to just wash over me.

When I let myself in, determined to rip the Band-Aid off and tell him how I've been feeling, I feared the worst-case scenario: that he would be weirded out by my very sudden, very unexpected (well, maybe not so unexpected, considering I've enjoyed sucking his cock) declaration of coming out and of loving him as more than a friend. I thought maybe he'd want to call off the relationship and ask for some space. I thought it might just be the event to put strain on our otherwise unbreakable friendship.

I am so glad that I was wrong.

I can't say I'm entirely surprised that my worst-case fears didn't eventuate. Jay *has* been right there with me as we 'helped each other out'. He's kissed me and jerked me off and, like I said earlier, straight men probably aren't going to be as into that as Jay and I have been.

God, we're a pair of Muppets, aren't we?

How could we not have seen it?

Except...Jay did, didn't he? He admitted that he's known he's had feelings for me —or at least a crush on me— since we were kids. My heart hurts that he thought he had to hide those feelings, that he never felt quite comfortable enough saying something...but, at the same time, I get it.

When we were kids, we didn't have the same self-confidence as we do now. Being anything other than straight was something joked about on the playground. It was taboo. *Gay* was a slur. While I want to say that I would have defended him to the ends of the earth, would fourteen or fifteen-year-old me have realised the potential that I might reciprocate his feelings? Probably not.

So, despite the potential loss of time together romantically, it's better that it has worked out this way. We're different people to those kids. Life and experience has moulded us into the men we are now. And, without those years and all that life stuff, Mia wouldn't exist.

I love that kid far too much to contemplate a life without her, and I'm not even her dad. I'm sure, given a choice, James wouldn't change being a parent, not even at nineteen.

"We are going to tell her, right?" James murmurs, cutting into my thoughts.

I shouldn't be surprised that he's also thinking about Mia, though in a very different way to me. We've always just been on the same wavelengths, or at least similar ones. It would be freaky if I didn't think it was just another sign that we work well together.

"Mmhmm," I breathe in his shampoo and try to pull him even closer against me. He's warm, and the night air is cool. Winter is coming, even if winters on the Gold Coast are what a lot of the world would consider t-shirt weather. "Yeah. We will. Whenever you're ready."

He snuggles down into the mattress, tucking his head under my chin. "Can we...can we give it a couple of weeks? Just to see how it all works with us? Now that we're aware that we're actually in a relationship and not just...pretending?"

"Pretending to pretend, you mean?" I can't help but taunt a little, quickly adding, "But, yeah, we can make sure that this is going to be a real thing."

"I mean, it's *new*," he says. "Coming out. Telling Mia. Telling our parents. Our friends. Colleagues..."

I give him a squeeze and a gentle "*Shh*." Then I press my lips to the shell of his ear, revelling in the tremble of anticipation that shoots through him. "Nobody's opinion on our sexuality or our relationship matters, baby. Not even Mia's. It *doesn't*." I insist when I feel him tense up. "Yes, Mia will be affected by us being together, but when have either of us ever not put her first? She will *always* be the priority for you, and for me. It doesn't make any difference if we're best friends or boyfriends. And our parents? Well," I consider how mine might react —surprise? confusion?— and I know in my gut that they'll support us even if they don't understand it. James' parents will be the same way. "They might need some time to wrap their heads around it, but they love us. Both of us. They'll probably be happy that we're not doomed to bachelorhood after all."

Letting out a shaky breath, James nods. "Yeah. Yeah, that's true. It just...it *feels* like a big deal. Like...like I've been lying to everyone about who I really am."

"You haven't."

"But—"

"You were a kid, James. Everyone goes through random crushes in their teens. I had a thing for Lola Bunny for a while."

"You...what?"

"The point is," I steamroll over the question, not needing to delve deeper into that embarrassing topic, "sexuality is fluid. I've read heaps of stories online about men not realising they like other men until they hit their fifties. *Fifties*, Jay. We're babies in comparison to that." Giving him an affectionate nudge with my nose, I finish with, "No matter what, we've got each other's backs, just like we always have. That's not going to change."

***

"You're sure about this?" James asks.

It has been the longest three days of my life. Three days since I declared my not-so-platonic love for my best friend. Three days since his teenage daughter cockblocked us from consummating our suddenly not-actually-fake relationship. Three days since I told James I wanted him to fuck me and then had to sleep with him in my arms without any sexy touches.

Three days of *torture*.

It's almost like my body and my brain have been on pins and needles, having the permission to do *all* the things with the man I love, only to not have the opportunity to act on my newfound freedom.

Between work commitments and Mia's after-school drama club stuff, getting a moment alone with James where we *haven't* been some form of exhausted has been impossible.

Until tonight.

Tonight, Mia is sleeping over at a friend's house. Tonight, James and I went on our first official date. Tonight, we have been flirting and teasing each other with light touches and 'come hither' eyes.

Tonight, I am splayed out in the middle of his bed, naked and aching for him, and he's equally naked and ready to move things along.

Except he has stopped, lube held in one hand and a condom in the other, and he's looking at me with nervous grey-green eyes and asking if *I'm* sure.

"I've never been more sure in my life," I tell him spreading my legs wider in invitation. "Please?"

I've showered and prepped already, wanting to make this experience as easy and stress-free as possible. Still, there's a nervous thrum under my skin, making my heart beat erratically.

This is new for me, too, and despite assuring James that we can make it work if this is a bust, I do worry that maybe we can't. That maybe he'll miss having a warm body to sink inside — or maybe even I will. On top of that, I've never had a dick inside me before. One of my ex girlfriends liked to play with my prostate when she was blowing me, but Jay's dick is much, much bigger than her slender fingers were.

Since I had my revelation that our relationship is real, I have been playing with myself, though. I haven't gone far enough to fuck myself on a fake cock, but I bought a set of plugs and tried stretching myself out with them.

It...wasn't my favourite thing ever. But then, I've always enjoyed sex more with a partner. Even jerking off on my own isn't as appealing. Isn't that what drove me to start the whole FWBs thing to begin with?

Maybe my subconscious was trying to tell me something from the very beginning.

So, yeah...I really want this to work out. I want tonight to be a success. I want—

"You're sure?"

"Jesus, Jay, I'm not some fifteen-year-old virgin. Get in bed and fuck me already."

"Can we not mention teenagers and fucking in the same sentence?" He complains, but starts crawling up from the foot of the bed, bringing his treasures with him.

I grab for him when he's within arm's reach and haul him down for a kiss, all my synapses lighting up at the feel of his naked skin rubbing against mine.

I love our contrasts.

He's pale and soft where I'm darker-toned and lean, his body hair light in colour and coverage where mine is dark and a bit more generous.

I discovered weeks ago that I love threading my fingers into his thick, mid-length hair, fascinated by the sensation seeing as I keep my own head shaved smooth (a curse of male-pattern baldness striking me in my late twenties, I'm afraid).

He has very light stubble, seeing as he shaves every morning, while I've got a beard and am contemplating growing it out from the short, neat style I keep it in.

We're yin and yang, and yet somehow we are so in sync that our parents used to joke that we were twins separated at birth.

That would make what we're about to do *really* taboo, I suppose.

Not that I'd ever judge someone's kinks. You do you, and all that jazz.

Focus, Evan.

As our leaking cocks rub together, I wind my legs around his hips, arching my back and moaning into our kiss. Any more teasing and I think I really might implode.

"What do I do here?" He asks through panted breaths. "And I swear to God, if you give me some smart-arse answer..."

I chuckle into the hanging silence of his unspoken threat and peck another kiss to his lips. "You know me too well." Before he can pull away, I give him the proper answer. "Condom on, lube up. Use the excess to stretch me out a little more — I did a bit of prep when I, uh, freshened up, but..." I lick my lips, feeling heat rise to my cheeks.

There are so many things I want to tell him. Things he already knows, like the fact that I've never done this before, like how much bigger his cock is than a couple of feminine fingers, like how badly I want to feel his fingers inside me, wanting to experience as much of him as possible tonight in case...

In case this doesn't work out.

"You'll tell me if I'm doing it wrong?"

"Baby," my heart thuds almost painfully at the earnest, vulnerable look on his face, "nothing you do to me could be wrong."

James sits back on his heels, forcing my legs to fall from their perch on his hips. I prop up on my elbows to greedily watch him rolling the condom over his dick, then swallow as he drizzles lube over his sheathed length and strokes.

"Fuck," I mutter, eyes glued to the motion, "that's hotter than any of the porn I've been watching."

A self-conscious blush spreads over his cheeks, then travels down his neck and the top of his chest. "I'm not exactly built like a pornstar." He gestures to the soft swell of his stomach. He describes his pooch as dad bod or a beer belly. I just think it makes him way more comfortable to cuddle.

I scoff. "They're not all cut abs and stuff," I tell him, thinking of the bears I've taken a liking to. "Besides, you're more than hung like one."

His blush gets deeper.

He's so fucking adorable.

I wriggle my hips. "Step two, baby. Don't skimp on the forepl—oh, God, yes."

My eyes practically roll back in their sockets as he takes his lubed fingers to my hole, tentatively rubbing at the rim before easing two in at once.

All I can think is 'Holy fuck, my best friend is inside me.'

Because, holy fuck, James is *inside* me.

As expected, his two fingers are a lot thicker than my ex's were. More cautious and exploratory, too. He takes his time, pushing them in slowly, scissoring them and curling them and—

"Holy mother of—fucking fuck," I cry, seeing stars as he strokes over *that* spot.

"Oh, Ev, Jesus..." he murmurs, stroking my prostate again, "look at you."

I can't. Firstly, because my eyes are squeezed shut. Secondly, because there's no mirror on the ceiling, and as much as I might joke that we share a brain, I can't see what he's seeing.

"You feel so tight and hot," he continues, still prodding at the magic button he's found. The constant stimulation is bordering on torture, but I'm enjoying it too much to tell him to stop. "I'm gonna come within seconds of getting inside you."

"You keep doing —ah! Fucking hell— *that*, and I'll come before you get the chance to get in me."

He stops abruptly.

I whine and open my eyes into slits to glare at him.

Jay stares back at me, wide eyed. "Is it really that good?"

"For me it is, yeah."

"M-maybe, y'know, the next time you blow me…"

I have to slam my eyes shut again at that mental imagery. "Jesus, baby, don't say stuff like that when I'm already so close." I arch my back as he starts to stretch me again, this time with a bit more confidence. I hiss at the burn, and he stops again. "Keep…keep going," I urge. "Your cock's gonna need more room than that."

"But it's hurting you."

"That'll pass." *I hope.* "Please, Jay, keep go—*oh.*"

Sure enough, he crooks his fingers and the pain is forgotten as the insane jolts of pleasure from having my prostate played with take over.

"Hmm," he sounds smug, but I still can't open my eyes, "that helps, huh?"

"*Nnnngghh.*"

"That's it," he encourages me as his fingers keep up their motion, "relax and let me in. You feel so good, Ev. You're gonna feel amazing around my cock."

The sweet praise makes me writhe. I want to feel good for him. I want this to be so fucking good that there's no question about our relationship working out — sexually, at least.

"I'm ready," I tell him, the words coming out breathy and needy. "Jay, please…" I try not to whine as he withdraws his fingers. Instead, I force my eyes open and prop myself up to watch him coat his already lubed condom with more of the slippery stuff, then wipe his hand on the sheets.

"Just to be sure," he says when he catches me watching, and I shake my head.

"I don't care. Just get it in me."

He shuffles forward and pushes the head of his cock inside me and *fuck*, it hurts. I breathe through it and try to bear down and relax, remembering the pleasure his fingers were giving me only a few moments ago. If I can get past the initial discomfort of having a *huge*, thick shaft penetrating me and filling me up, I know it's going to be good. More than good.

Why the fuck didn't I practice with a dildo?

"Fuck, Ev," he pants as he inches inside me in excruciating short rocking motions, "you're *tight*. I haven't…it's been a *long* time since I've, uh, been inside someone and…*oh God*, don't *clench*."

"It…wasn't…deliberate…" I respond defensively. I'm afraid that if I give away just how uncomfortable the intrusion is, he'll pull out. I'm not doing a good job of keeping it from him, though. I can tell because he stills suddenly.

"Are you okay?"

"I'm fine. Keep—"

"Evan," his tone is firm. Demanding. It *does things* to me.

Swallowing, I open my watering eyes. His widen with horror and I scramble to hold him in place, crying out when my action of wrapping my legs around his hips drives him deeper inside me.

"Ev —shit, fuck, Jesus— are you…" he trails off, pausing for breath, then fumbles forward to grab one of my hands, lacing our fingers together beside my head on the mattress, "are you okay?"

Now that he's further inside me, my body is acclimatising. I nod.

James carefully lowers his lips to mine and kisses me slowly, distracting me from the remaining pain. I melt into his kiss, the tension in my shoulders loosening. His tongue teases mine, coaxing me to relax further. We groan into each other's mouths as he slides the rest of the way inside me, his balls tickling my arse.

His hand squeezes mine and he ends the kiss to murmur, "I knew you'd feel amazing."

I hum my agreement, the burn and near-stabbing pain of his initial push inside finally turning to a more pleasant ache. It's still accompanied by a mild feeling of wrongness —of my body trying to tell me that that particular orifice is *not* an intake point— but that's fading, too.

"You can—you can *move*," I tell him. "Please move."

It becomes more enjoyable again when he resumes kissing me, slowly easing his cock out and then back inside me. Once he's got a rhythm going, I start arching up to meet him. It's still not the most amazing experience of my life, but it's James, and it's *us*, and— "Oh my God, right there. Do that again!" I tear my mouth from his to make the demand.

That. That burst of fireworks in my veins. That intense jolt of bliss. *That* is why men rave about being fucked like this. *That* is what I'm going to crave more of.

Jay moves again, making small, pleasured grunts and '*ungh*' sounds every time he bottoms out. He misses the mark more than he hits it, but as he starts to pick up the pace, hiking my legs higher up his waist and changing up the angle, I get more and more into it.

I reach for my dick, stroking it back to full hardness between our bodies as James pistons in and out of me.

"Ev," he pants, "E-Ev. I'm...I'm gonna..."

"No-no-no-no-no-no," I whine, finally feeling myself enjoying this properly. "I'm not there yet."

"I know," I glance up to find his face scrunched up with concentration and apology, his jaw clenched and sweat dripping down his temples. "B-but you're so *tight* and I—*fuck*, honey, I can't…I can't…I'm coming. Fuck. I'm, oh…*fuck*."

He stops moving, his hips stuttering as his already thick cock swells and then explodes deep inside me. The rapture on his pink face is worth the disappointment of not going over the edge before him, and I do my best not to wince when he grips the base of the condom around his softening cock and withdraws.

He ties it off and chucks it over the side of the bed, then surprises me by shuffling backwards down the mattress.

"Where are you—" I start, then suck in a sharp *"Oh, fuck,"* as he sinks his mouth down over my cock.

I *have* to watch this. My arms feel shaky as I push up on my elbows, but I *have* to see him. He's uncoordinated and sloppy, but *oh, God*, his mouth feels like heaven. Watching his luscious, flopsy blond hair flying every which way as his head bobs up and down on my dick is a sight I will commit to memory.

"Jay, baby, that's so good," I tell him, torn between lying back to free my arms so I can thread my fingers through his hair, or staying propped up so I can watch my dick disappearing into plump, pink, spit-slicked lips. Then he *sucks*, and I think I go cross-eyed. "Holy—*oh, Christ…*"

He brings a hand to my still lubricated, thoroughly stretched hole and *plunges* three fingers into me, seeking out my prostate with startling accuracy.

I *howl* at the competing sensations. The warmth and wetness of his mouth. The suction. The stretch of his fingers. The nearly electric bursts of bliss as he strokes my prostate.

It's too much.

It's so good.

It's so much, too good.

"J-Jay…"

He releases his grip around the base of my cock and fondles my balls, adding an additional sensation to the mix.

My brain explodes. Or, at least, it feels like it does. With my eyes shut —and I have no idea when *that* happened— I see stars. Someone is shouting incomprehensibly, and I have the strangest feeling that it's me. Blood roars in my ears, which should be impossible seeing as my body's supply was being routed to my cock, and I'm shaking, *trembling* as I come down from the most intense orgasm I've had in my whole life.

I barely register the mattress bouncing beneath me as James crawls back up along my side. His hands smooth over my body, gentling the adrenaline shakes.

"You with me yet, honey?" he asks, and I'm surprised that my own chuckle sounds watery and weak.

Did I…was I *crying*?

"I like it when you call me honey," I tell him, the words coming out all mumbled and jumbled.

James kisses the back of my head, then my temple, then my cheek. I snuggle up against his bare chest, my eyelids drooping.

"Go to sleep," he urges, then yawns himself. "That was…"

"Yeah," I agree. "I love you."

Even though it's even more garbled than my previous sentence, he seems to understand. His arms tighten around me, and his lips ghost over the shell of my ear. "I love you, too, Ev."

Chapter Thirteen

James

"You're the actual best," I tell Ev as I toss my overnight bag into the backseat of my car. "I tried to get them to send Moira, but—"

"Baby, it's fine," he soothes, then stills my anxious movements by placing flattened palms over my chest. "You're gone for two nights. Pretty sure I can keep your sixteen-year-old alive until you get back. She's easier to look after than that godforsaken houseplant you had." Sighing, he shakes his head. "I still don't know what you were thinking getting a *plant*."

"Funny, most people find plants easier to keep an eye on than children."

As usual, he's managed to ease my anxiety with a few words and a smile.

When Collin told me that I had been chosen to represent our firm to our largest client, I'd been thrilled. It was my campaign pitch which had won them over, after all, so it made sense that I head up the planning meetings. Except, the client demanded that the meetings happen in person, at their head office in Sydney, and there was no way I could get out of the three-day work trip.

Thank God I have a boyfriend who loves my kid as much as I do. He volunteered to say with her for the two nights I'll be gone without me needing to even ask.

We've been together —really, officially together— for just over a month now, and nothing between us has really changed. We're more affectionate with each other, and we're not pretending that the orgasms we're sharing are just 'bros helping bros', but...that's it. We still hang out and watch sports together, still share beers and talk shit, and still go out for dinner and drinks just like we used to. We just...kiss now. Hold hands. Play footsie. It's like the missing piece in our friendship has been filled.

Not that either of us knew there was a missing piece to start with. We're just...closer now.

"You sure you don't want me to drive you to the airport and pick you up on Thursday?" he asks, shaking me out of my musings.

"Nah. Work is covering all my expenses. Might as well make them cover the exorbitant parking, too, right? No sense making you come get me when I get in at stupid-o'clock on Thursday, either."

Evan pouts exaggeratedly and tugs me in by my beltloops. "It just means I have to wait that little bit longer to see you again."

"Oh my God, you're ridiculous," I laugh, and he cracks up, too. Then he swats my butt and gives me the shooing motion.

"Go," he says, "I've got this. I promise Mia will still be in once piece when you get home."

"My plant was still in one piece," I grumble. "Just drowned."

"I promise not to drown Mia." It's the exaggerated, nearly-teenaged way he says it that gets me laughing again.

"You'd better not," I point my index finger at him sternly. "We can't make a replacement."

His grin turns positively wicked. "But we can *try*. Come back soon and practice knocking me up, Jay. Oh, hi, Mrs. Wakerley." He waves over my shoulder.

I feel heat climbing up my neck and over my face as I turn to find my elderly neighbour frozen at her mailbox. Her cheeks are pink, and she's clutching her fuzzy lavender-coloured bathrobe tightly at her chest.

God, I hope we haven't scandalised her into a heart attack...

"Hi," I practically squeak, offering her a wave of my own.

"I didn't hear anything," she says, snatching up her mail and shuffling back up the path to her front door. Then, right before she shuts the door, she adds, "Be safe, boys!"

Evan loses it. His laughter is loud and infectious, and soon neither of us can breathe.

"You're *awful*," I tell him through wheezing breaths, tears blurring my vision. "I'll never be able to look her in the eye again."

"That" —he points in the direction of Mrs. Wakerley's shut front door— "sounded like a ringing endorsement to me."

He really is *so* ridiculous.

God, I love him.

"You'll miss your flight if you don't head off soon," he says, interrupting my moment of mooning over him.

Shit.

"Right. *Ugh*. Behave," I tell him. "And call me if you have any issues. If I have to get an earlier flight back, I will."

"We'll be *fine*," he insists, planting his hands on his hips. "I've scheduled the house parties to end at ten p.m. Mia will be tucked in bed by curfew."

"You're not cute," I tell him, then lean in to peck my lips to his. I gasp as he grabs my hips and yanks me in, deepening the kiss. My cock twitches in my jeans —a Pavlovian response to his kisses at this point— and I pull away reluctantly. "I've gotta go. I love you."

"I love you," he replies. "Let me know when you've landed safe and sound. I'll see you Thursday night."

***

"I can't believe they only booked one room," I mutter, placing my overnight bag on one of the twin beds in the hotel room booked for the trip.

Andi drops hers on the matching bed and then sits down on it, bouncing in place, presumably testing its firmness. "Is it really so bad rooming with me for a couple of nights?" she teases. "We're both adults here."

Yeah, I think uncharitably. *And I was hoping to at least have phone sex with my boyfriend.*

I certainly won't be doing that in a shared room.

Suddenly, two nights apart feels like *forever*.

Dear God, I sound like Mia.

"I just like my privacy," I tell her, because it's rude not to reply, and I don't want to start this trip by upsetting my project partner. I force a smile her way. "I've gotten used to it."

Andi snorts. "I would think you'd *enjoy* having a single woman sharing a bed —*er*— *room* with you after years of being single yourself." She flops onto her bed, then rolls onto her side and bats her lashes at me.

I laugh at her antics. "That's a HR drama waiting to happen," I snicker, then pull out my phone to text Ev as promised. "Good one, though."

Andi grunts and gets back up off her bed. "I'm going to get changed," she declares, a hint of annoyance in her tone. "Then we can get a taxi over for meeting number one."

Ah, that explains the annoyance: client meetings are the worst. All the brown nosing and pandering we have to do...I hate it. I just want to plan marketing campaigns and analyse data. Everything else is just frustrating. I'm sure Andi feels the same way.

"I'll make sure all the presentation stuff is ready to go," I call after her.

She doesn't answer.

My phone lights up in my hand with Ev's reply.

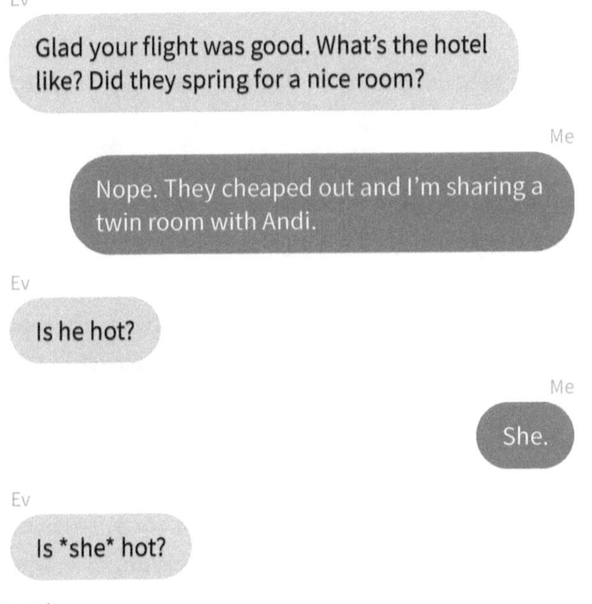

I snort.

Evan sends me back a string of emojis, including 'the finger' and the emoji poking out its tongue and squinting.

I reply with a blown kiss emoji and look up as Andi clears her throat. I must have missed her coming back out of the bathroom. She arches an eyebrow at me. "We good to go?" she still sounds a bit miffed.

I slide my phone into my pocket and nod. "Yep." Slinging my laptop bag over my shoulder, I smile at her and sweep my hand towards the door. "Ladies first."

She rolls her eyes, and I smother a sigh. *Great.* It's going to be a long-arse couple of days if she's going to be in a mood the whole time.

"So," I ask as I follow her down the hallway, after double checking that our hotel room door definitely locked when I shut it, "are you seeing anyone?"

"I *just* told you I was single," she huffs.

It starts to dawn on me that *maybe* her mood hasn't got anything to do with work. I pause mid-stride. "I'm sorry, I was a little distracted earlier." I was too concerned with texting Evan when we were talking, and now I feel guilty. Maybe I owe her a bit more of an explanation. "I, um..." I stall, not sure what to say.

It hits me that I might just be about to come out for the first time, and I'm not sure how to feel about it. Nervous? Yeah, I'm a bit nervous. But also relieved. Excited, even. Because I love Evan, and there's a part of me that wants to shout about our relationship from the rooftops.

But, at the same time, it's still so new, and so different. And we haven't even told Mia yet. We came close at the end of the school holidays, when we were rostered to assist with the drama department's after school rehearsals for the musical, but in the end we opted against it. Maybe I was being too cautious, but I want to be able to sit down and talk it out properly with her, not just drop the bomb without giving her adequate processing time.

"Um?" Andi prompts with folded arms from a few feet away, drumming her fingernails over her biceps.

She arches an eyebrow, and I confess, "I've started dating someone. It's...new. And a bit different."

Andi's expression seems to flicker through a variety of reactions —not all of which I can place— before she gapes at me with wide eyes.

It's not *that* surprising, is it? I mean, I haven't even said I'm dating a man. I kept it all gender neutral.

"Well, shit," she says, and I blink.

"What?"

Her pale, freckled cheeks turn a deep red, matching her hair. "God, I'm sorry, James. I was flirting with you." Her cheeks darken further while I try to come to terms with *that* revelation. "I just threw myself at you back there and everything." She waves her hand in the vague direction of our hotel room. "I'm so embarrassed."

"You...wait...what?"

Exactly how long has this been going on? I've never noticed any flirting. *How* could I have not noticed?

Andi's a really attractive woman. With her wild red hair and porcelain skin, and ample curves, she's got a natural sensual vibe about her. I mean, yeah, she's joked about us dating before but...

Oh, God, I'm a moron.

The joking was her flirting. She was coming on to me, and I was cracking jokes about HR violations.

I want to facepalm.

Covering her face with her hands, she shakes her head. "Can we just forget all of this ever happened?"

"I...yeah, sure." I have no idea what else to say, or how else to handle the whole situation. "For what it's worth, I'm sorry I was so oblivious..."

No, not oblivious. Distracted.

By Evan.

A buxom, beautiful woman has been throwing herself at me for months, and I've been too wrapped up in Ev to notice.

He's going to get a kick out of that.

"You're *such* a man," she chuckles, and even though it's an awkward attempt to break past the tension of whatever the fuck this past few minutes has been, I grab onto it and run.

"I am. You need to be *way* more blatant with me, Andi. I'm dumb and oblivious."

She snorts and finally things between us start to feel normal again. "Can I record you saying that?" she asks, and we start to head towards the elevators again. "I want to make it my ringtone."

"Nope, you missed your chance."

I catch her wince out of the corner of my eye. She sighs as she presses the call button for the lift. "In more ways than one, apparently."

Okay, maybe the tension isn't all gone.

"Andi..."

She waves my attempted apology off. "No, it's my bad. I should have realised you weren't picking up the signs." Giving me a little smile, she leans over and bumps my bicep with her shoulder. The lift *dings* as the carriage arrives and the doors slide open. It's empty and, as we step inside, she prods, "So...tell me about her."

"Who?"

"Jesus, you really are dense, aren't you? *Her.* The woman who snapped you up right out from under my nose."

I swallow roughly, feeling my heart rate pick up. Butterflies beat their wings in my belly, and I wonder why I ever thought it was a good idea to bring up my love life to begin with. "She, um," my stomach swoops as the elevator descends, and hesitate again. "She's a he, actually. Ev. Um, Evan. It's...it's Evan."

The doors swish open at the ground floor, but Andi stands in place, staring at me as if she's seeing me for the first time.

I guess she kind of is. The *real* me, anyway. The me who has been infatuated and half-in-love with his best friend for decades.

An older guy clears his throat, clearly wanting to get into the lift, and that's enough to shake Andi out of her stupor. She apologises and hurries out into the hotel foyer, and I follow after her, also muttering an apology to the man as we pass.

"Evan?" she asks as we make our way out through the reception area and to the pickup and drop off zone. "As in...your best friend?"

Still feeling a little sick with nerves, I nod. "The one and same. I'll, uh, book us an Uber, yeah?"

I pull out my phone and bring up the Uber app, plugging in the details for our trip while I feel Andi's gaze boring into me. The app tells me a driver will be with us in three minutes. Three long, agonisingly awkward minutes.

"Done," I tell her, fingers itching to type an SOS message to my boyfriend.

"Wow," my colleague shakes her head. "Well, I can't exactly compete with a dick, can I?" She grins at me. "They're pretty awesome, huh?"

What the hell is happening?

"I…"

Looping her arm in mine, Andi gives my bicep a squeeze. "I'm going to need to hear the whole friends-to-lovers story," she continues to chat happily, completely unaware of my brain melting down at the turn the conversation has taken. "It's so sweet. And, *oh*, you've known him since you were kids, right? So he's also been there for Mia's whole life…it's *so* romantic!"

Ignoring the fact that I haven't told her our getting together story, I nod. "It kind of is, yeah. Took us both by surprise, but" —a goofy smile works its way across my face— "yeah."

"I'm so happy for you, James. Really." She gives my bicep another squeeze. "Am I the first person you've told?"

"Am I that obvious?"

"I mean…you just seemed really nervous, but that could have been because I was propositioning you all of fifteen minutes ago." She cringes. "Sorry again about that."

"I'm sorry I was too wrapped up in what's been going on with Ev to notice. If things were different…"

"Oh," she blinks as our Uber pulls into the hotel's driveway, "you're still into women?"

"Uh, yeah. I'm bi, not gay."

Her red, lipstick covered lips draw up into a smirk, and she playfully teases, "Then maybe I can compete with him after all."

Something inside me settles at how easily she rolls with my coming out. Like it's not a huge deal. I laugh and shake my head. "Nah; I think he's the one."

The Uber pulls up and, as I open the front passenger door, confirming my name with the driver, I gesture for Andi to take the seat. She hesitates and softly says, "Thank you for trusting me with this, James. I'm honestly honoured that I'm the first person you've told."

Then she slides into her seat, and I take the one behind her, the conversation ended now that we're in the car.

My heart feels lighter, and I can't help but grab for my phone to text Ev.

Me

I just came out to Andi.

It went well.

I think we can tell Mia now. And our parents.

I get his reply just as we pull up to the client's building twenty minutes later.

Ev

I'm so proud of you, baby. As soon as you come home, we'll tell the whole world.

There's no sense of anxiety over that promise. Instead, all I feel is excitement and a sense of rightness.

I tuck my phone back into my pocket and head into the meeting with a huge smile on my face.

The future is looking bright.

Chapter Fourteen

Evan

Mia is much easier to look after than a potted plant, mostly because not only is she able to communicate her needs, she's also sixteen-years-old and perfectly capable of feeding herself and taking herself off to the bathroom and such. So, unsurprisingly, Tuesday night goes by without any drama at all.

When I'm tucked away in Jay's guest room (because it was easier than trying to explain crashing in Jay's bed), I do regret that the sheets here smell like clean linen and not my boyfriend, and that I can't even call him or text him for phone sex because he's sharing a room with his colleague.

His colleague who he came out to.

I'm surprised that he did, but also thrilled, too. Not that I thought I was going to remain his dirty little secret, but I'm champing at the bit to tell everyone how happy I am with him. How happy and stupidly in love I am with him.

He's taken the first brave step by telling his colleague and work friend, and he's opened the door for me to do the same. *And* he said that we can tell Mia and our parents, which makes it all feel so much more serious and real, but in all the best ways.

I *really* wish he wasn't sharing a room with his colleague right now, because just thinking about him being so confident in our relationship has me getting a little hot under the collar.

I want to call him. To hear his sexy voice. To whisper all my filthy thoughts down the phone line and listen to him pant and swear as we both jerk ourselves off.

My cock swells at the very idea of it.

I tug myself loose from my pj pants and, after spitting in my palm, I stroke my dick to full hardness. Then, in a moment of genius, I grab my phone and snap a dick pic. Then, without any hesitation, I send it to him.

The bubbles of his reply appear almost immediately, followed by a barrage of quick-fire texts.

I chuckle and consider how I should respond.

She's already hit on me once today. I don't need her getting the wrong idea.

Wait...what?!

My fingers fly over my phone's keyboard.

What do you mean she's hit on you today?

Like, seriously hit on you?

I can see the ellipsis bubbles for his reply as I rapidly fire my questions at him.

While you're practically sleeping in the same bed??

This was before she knew I was in a relationship.

His responses come back as quickly as my questions.

I was oblivious.

She was mortified.

And we're sharing a room with separate beds.

While I'm still contemplating that, he sends another message. It stills my racing heart, soothing some of the panic.

Jay

Please tell me you're not actually freaking out right now. You've never been a jealous wanker before.

I reread the message and chuckle, feeling mildly sheepish. He's right. I'm acting like a real tosser.

When I message him again, it's with complete honesty.

Me

I've never been in love before.

James' bubbles appear and disappear before his final message comes through.

Jay

I've only ever been in love with you, Ev.

***

I'm still riding the high from James' sweet message by the time Thursday morning rolls around. We've texted on and off for the couple of nights that he's been gone, but I can't wait to hold him in my arms and kiss him within an inch of his life. So sue me if that sounds sappy: he started it.

Around ten a.m., my office is evacuated due to an issue with the security system, and I opt to head back to Jay's place to finish my day's work there. There's no point going to my sad, dated, cramped apartment at the back of Burleigh when his bright, airy house in Palm Beach is just waiting for me, after all. Not when this is where

I told Jay I'd meet him tonight, after his flight gets in from Sydney at stupid late o'clock.

I'm setting myself up at the kitchen bench, logging into my VPN on my laptop, when a sound filters in from the direction of the bedrooms.

James doesn't have pets. He doesn't even have plants anymore (not after the disaster of my last attempt at house sitting).

I lean back on my bar stool and listen intently.

It's a strange sort of sound. Muffled and distorted, but something like a...howl, maybe?

Worried that I might have left the laundry door open and an animal of some kind has gotten inside, I climb off my stool to investigate.

James will kill me if some neighbourhood cat has pissed on his carpet.

The closer I get to the hallway leading to the bedrooms, the louder the sound seems. I hesitate, trying to determine where it's coming from, and I determine that it's coming from Mia's room at the far end of the hallway.

Great. I can't imagine a sixteen-year-old girl is going to enjoy having to deal with whatever mess a stray creature trapped in her room has made.

Hoping that it is only a cat or something easy to deal with, I take a fortifying breath and swing Mia's bedroom door open...and then I freeze.

It's not an animal. It's Mia.

What the actual fuck?

Her pretty face red and blotchy, eyes swollen from crying, she hiccups mid-sob, just as startled to see me as I am to see her.

"W-what are you doing here?" she demands in a raspy, gravelly voice.

"*Me?!*" I sound equally as incredulous as I stare back at her. "What are *you* doing home?"

I dropped her off at school as usual at eight on the dot. I waved her off and watched her saunter up the manicured, winding path surrounded by hedges of some fancy-pants plant just as I've done countless times since Jay and I started our fake-but-actually-real relationship.

Then, coming to the conclusion that she's obviously playing hooky, I pat down my pockets, looking for my phone. Surely the school would have noticed and would have called Jay at the very least.

"I...um...I called the office and pretended I was Dad. Told them I was sick." Her lips lift at the corners. "They bought my acting." Her expression falls and then she starts sobbing again.

I have no idea what to do right now.

"Your impressions must be getting better," I acknowledge, before realising that I am, for all intents and purposes, her stepdad and if James was here, he'd be having kittens over her actions. "But, uh, not good, Mimi."

Yeah...my 'stern parent' voice needs work.

Her lower lip quivers. "Don't tell Dad. Please. I—" She sniffles and chokes on another sob. "He's going to hate me as it is."

"*Whoa.*" I'm shaking my head and stepping further into the room on instinct, sitting down beside her on her bed and wrapping my arm around her shoulders as I add, "Jay could never —*would never*— hate you, Mia. Never. Not even if you killed someone." I suck in a breath. "Please tell me you haven't killed anyone, though."

"No." The word comes out sounding both pouty and amused, but it's drowned by another garbled wail. She turns in my embrace and buries her face in the crook of my neck and mumbles words that I'm *sure* I misinterpret.

Heart racing and arms tightening on reflex, I ask, "Can you repeat that?"

Mia inhales shakily, then says exactly what I was afraid she would. "I might be pregnant." Then she breaks down, bawling loudly, and my brain struggles to come back online.

Okay, I think to myself, *this is slightly worse than what happened with the potted plant.*

Not that I'm responsible for...for...well, *y'know.*

Jesus, I'm thirty-five-year-old. I can say the 'p' word.

I just don't want to.

Because Mia is only sixteen. She's a baby herself. She's *Jay's* baby.

"Shh," I soothe, rubbing her back and rocking her a bit like when she was little. "It's going to be okay, Mimi, I promise."

"You can't promise that!" she wails.

"Yeah, I can. Because, no matter what, your dad loves you. I love you. And, hey, he was only two years older than you are now when he had to have this conversation with your grandparents and oh, God, that puts this into a whole different context..."

I actually feel a little bit sick thinking about it.

Jay was *so* young. He must have been so scared, just like Mia is now. Scared, stressed, unsure...

"H-he's going to be so m-mad."

I squeeze her a bit tighter. "He's not." *At least, he won't let it show.* "But, sweetheart, you...you said *might.* Do you know for sure? Like, have you taken a test, or...?"

Finally pulling back, she shakes her head and bites her lip. "I'm too embarrassed to buy one. What if...what if someone sees me?"

My heart goes out to her. She sounds so impossibly young right now.

Nodding, I say, "Okay. I'll go buy a couple. Best to cover our bases, right?" Then I lick my lips anxiously and ask, "Can I ask *why* you think you might be...?"

"My period is late. A-and my boobs are tender." Oh, God, I don't need to think about my goddaughter's boobs. "And I had gastro last month."

I frown. "You think that was morning sickness?"

"No." She sighs, then eyes me warily. "Did you know that vomiting and...other gastro symptoms...can impact the effectiveness of the Pill?"

"Nope. I did not know that."

"Well, it can. So can taking antibiotics."

I nod at that. I'm pretty sure that's how Mia came to be. Or, at least, that was what James said her mum's doctor had told them.

"Okay," I exhale, my heart hammering. "Okay. Well, I'll, uh, I'll head off to Woolies. Or the chemist. Uh, do you think the ones from the chemist would be better?" I pull out my phone and Google the question, feeling so very out of my depth.

Out of the corner of my eye, I watch Mia shrug. "They're all the same brands, right? But...maybe get a couple of different brands?"

"Yeah," I swallow. "Yeah, okay. Good plan."

I look back down at my phone and bite my lip. Should I call James? He'd get on an earlier flight home for an emergency like this. Except getting here earlier isn't going to change whatever the test results say, is it? And he'd just stress for the entire flight and taxi ride back home.

Deciding not to involve him until we at least have test results, I slide the device back into my pocket. Then I press my lips to the top of Mia's blonde head, reassuring her, "It'll be okay. No matter what, sweetheart, I promise."

***

The tests are inconclusive. I bought three in three different brands which all alluded to being some kind of early-response test, and Mia scurried into the bathroom with them as soon as I handed the bag over.

She was pale and shaking when she came back out, frowning at them in her trembling hands.

The digital one reads 'Negative'. One of the older-fashioned 'two line' tests hasn't even come up with the control line, making it null and void, but the third has what looks like —from certain angles, anyway— a very faint second line.

Fuck.

Mia's big, blue eyes are wide and wet as she looks up at me. "What do I do?"

Heart thumping madly, I take the tests, drop them into a ziplocked bag, and tell her I'll take her to her usual GP. When I call the clinic, the receptionist must hear the anxiety in my voice, because an appointment opens up miraculously for us.

Despite my nerves, I get us to the clinic in one piece. We're distracted on our walk through the busy car park, though, and I have to yank Mia back to my side when some guy in an SUV zooms past us in his haste to find a spot. Distractedly, I give him the finger and shout after his car for him to slow the hell down. He almost hit us! People around here always drive like they're the only ones on the road, even in parking lots like this one.

I don't usually lose my temper, but I was already shaken. Still, I should know better to keep my wits about me, especially when I'm supposed to be keeping my Goddaughter safe.

With my heart hammering from the close call, I'm even more anxious by the time I get Mia into the clinic, and she refuses to let go of my hand when her doctor calls her name.

I get an arched eyebrow from the woman as I take the spare seat in her office, her gaze flicking down to where Mia's hand is holding on to mine for dear life.

"Hi," I greet with an awkward smile. Doctor Miranda Rogers is about my age, with dark hair and a sharp, intense aura about her. She has pronounced cheekbones and a long, thin nose. She's very attractive, and also incredibly intimidating right now. "I'm Evan."

"And you're here with Mia because...?"

"He's my godfather."

"I'm engaged to her dad."

Mia and I answer at the same time, and Mia gives me a questioning look for a moment before turning back to her doctor, adding, "Dad's in Sydney for work."

At least Doctor Rogers seems a little more relaxed by my presence now. She nods, then offers Mia a softer expression. "So, what brings you here today?"

Mia squeezes my hand tightly and pulls the plastic bag of tests from her cross-body handbag. "I took these earlier and I still don't know..."

Great. Neither of us can say it out loud, apparently.

Without a hint of judgment, the doctor takes the tests and examines them through the bag. She sets the bag down on her desk and then turns back to Mia. "Alright, well, a blood test is going to be the most effective way to determine whether you're pregnant or not. But, first, let's run through the reasons why you think you might be, okay?"

Mia nods. I feel like an intruder as she answers the questions, which are pretty standard. When was her last period, did she miss any pills, has she had any symptoms, when did she have sex, and: "Did you use a condom?"

I close my eyes and try very hard not to react when Mia winces and shakes her head.

That, I think, *James will be pissed about.*

He'll probably also go apeshit over her having sex at all, but to not use a condom? Ignoring the risk of pregnancy, what about the risk of STIs?

"I *know*," Mia says, and it takes me a second to realise that she's talking to me. I glance at her to find her looking at her feet, scuffing the toes of her school shoes over the speckled linoleum floor. "I know how dumb that was. But...but he didn't have any and I *really* liked him and—"

"I remember being sixteen," I surprise myself with how calm I sound, even if my voice is a little strangled. "I did some stupid shit, too. You know it wasn't the best choice; I'm not going to yell at you for it. That won't change anything."

Your dad, on the other hand...

Mia launches over the armrests of our respective chairs, hugging me as she starts to cry all over again, and I catch the doctor's eye over her shoulder. The look on the woman's face is one of approval, and I find that oddly reassuring.

This step-parenting thing is *way* harder than I thought it would be.

Chapter Fifteen

James

The first sign I get that something is rotten in the state of Denmark is the absolute lack of contact from my boyfriend all day on Thursday. The second sign is the almost distracted *'U 2'* I receive when I finally give in and text him to say I'm on my way back and I miss him. But the third, and final, sign is the tension I can feel when I let myself into my own home.

It's silent, but not in a comfortable 'everyone is asleep' way. I don't know how I can tell the difference, but I can. Call it a parent's intuition, or something. I drop my keys and wallet in the bowl on the sidetable in the entryway, and then just about leap out of my skin when I walk into the living room to find Evan hunched over on the couch in the dark.

"Jesus Christ," I hiss at him, "what the fuck, Ev?"

With his elbows braced on his thighs, and his hands clasped together in an approximation of prayer or begging, he raises his forehead from where it was resting on his hands and looks up at me with a similar serious expression to the one he used when he told me that he had feelings for me.

"You're going to want to sit," he says, and he doesn't even sound like himself.

I plant my feet and demand, "What's going on?"

"Jay," even the way he says my name is eerily calm and foreboding, "sit down."

Dropping my overnight bag on the floor, I do as I'm told, taking the spot beside him. He swivels sideways and reaches for my hand, holding it tightly. In the dim light from the outside streetlight, I watch as his eyes line with concern and hesitation behind his sexy glasses frames.

"What's wrong?" I ask. The anxiety which has been slowly churning in my gut since I realised he wasn't texting me today is now turning to dread. "Ev?"

"Fuck, I've had hours to think about how to drop this on you and I just don't..."

"Evan," tugging gently at his hand, I try to soothe his nerves even while mine are all sitting on knifepoint.

I have the strangest feeling that he's going to break up with me. Tell me that he was wrong: that he can't imagine being in a relationship with a man —with me— for the long-haul. That he misses women, or that he wants...something else. He's had time away from me to realise that he was just infatuated with the novel experience, or whatever.

Even though it hurts to think, I'd rather he get it out now, while we have a chance of salvaging our friendship, than if he continues to drag things out.

"Just...say it," I prompt.

He takes a deep breath. I brace myself. "Mia might be pregnant." He winces as he delivers the news.

"Wh-*what?!*" I was braced for a breakup. I was *not* braced for that.

I surge to my feet, intent on racing to her room to…I don't even know what. Ask her what the hell she was thinking? Hold her and tell her it's scary but it will be okay? Demand that she tell me that this is some really piss-weak practical joke?

Ev gently pulls me back down to the couch, shaking his head. "She's asleep. It's been a rough day."

"No shit," I scoff with liberal sarcasm. Scrubbing my hand over my face, I narrow my eyes at him and demand, "Tell me everything. *Now.*"

Squeezing my hand again, he does. I get the run down about how he discovered her in her room, distraught. Just hearing it breaks my heart, as does his admission that she told him that I would hate her.

"I promise," he assures me, his wobbly voice emphatic, "I told her there was no chance of that happening. I don't even think she believed it herself. She was just scared. Is still scared."

"I wasn't here," I lament, guilt roiling my stomach. "She was freaking out and I wasn't here."

"But I was. I still am." Ev's words calm me and soothe some of the ache in my heart. "And you're here *now*. And now is going to be the hardest part because we're stuck in limbo waiting for the blood test results."

"Blood tests?"

"Oh, right. I didn't get that far yet." He sighs wearily, then launches into the rest of his story. Of going to buy her tests, of them being inconclusive, of taking her to the doctor. He winces again. "She wanted me in there with her. Moral support or whatever. But some of those questions…"

I can remember going to Haley's —Mia's mother's— early appointments with her almost as if it was yesterday. It wasn't even seventeen years ago, so it's no wonder the memories still feel vivid. I scrunch my nose and nod.

"...So, yeah," he continues, "then the doctor sent her off for blood tests, including a whole panel for STIs and stuff, and it'll be a couple of days before we know. I, uh, I called the school and told them she was still sick and would be out the rest of the week. I'm sorry if that was overstepping, but—"

"No," I interrupt him, "no, that's perfect. *You're* perfect. I hate that I wasn't here, but I'm glad you were."

"And I'm sorry I didn't call or text you. I..." Ev licks his lips and looks me in the eye. "This was something I thought was better said in person."

"Yeah," I breathe, my mind feeling like it's moving through molasses. It's slow to function, too many thoughts and emotions churning through it at once. "Yeah, I get it. I'm not mad. Not at you. Not at her. But...fuck," I tighten my grip on his hand, panic starting to set in. "What do we do if she is?"

"What did your parents do for you?"

"Loved me. Supported me. Adored Mia."

"Then we do that. But," he levels me with another serious look, his stare so sharp and piercing behind his frames that it takes my breath away, "we're not influencing her decision. It's her body. If she chooses not to go through with the pregnancy..."

I'm nodding even before he trails off. "Of *course*," I tell him, a little horrified that he'd think otherwise. He knows me better than that. "Whatever she chooses, I will love her and support her."

"And, uh," Ev swallows again, this time a little nervous, "if...and I mean *if* she chooses to put the baby up for adoption..." I can feel his hand trembling in mine, and I don't quite understand until he takes a steadying breath and finishes, "…I think *we* should consider adopting it."

I was not braced for that, either.

Chapter Sixteen

Evan

"**S**ay *something*," I come just short of begging. "Please, baby."

Baby. That word —that endearment— feels a little more loaded now.

"You don't think that's moving too fast?" Jay eventually asks me, sounding just as blindsided as he looks.

"Honestly? It is. But hear me out," I rush to add, wanting to smooth away the furrows in his handsome brow, "I've been thinking about this all day. And, even if it is too fast, I can't see myself settling down with anyone else. I...I wouldn't *plan* to have kids other than Mia herself, but I think...I mean, with *you*, I'd...I'd want that. Because that baby would be a tiny bit you, too. And Mia herself is awesome and I've *really* been overthinking this." I finish with an awkward chuckle, rubbing the back of my neck.

James slumps against the back of the couch, blinking at me with a stunned expression. "Wow. That's..." he clears his throat. "That's intense, Ev. Not necessarily in a bad way, just...well, it's a lot. And babies are..." He trails off again and licks his lips. "They test you, you know? Like, I know I raised Mia by myself, but I know so many couples who struggled to stay together under the pressure of having no sleep and all the other baby-related stress and I...I'm selfish, Evan. I don't want to lose you."

"That's not selfish," I assure him. I shuffle in close to his side and wrap my arm around his shoulders, squeezing him tightly. "You've done the baby thing before, and if it's not something you ever want to do again, I'm good with that. I just...I just wanted to put the option out there. Let you know it's something we can consider. Y'know, if it comes to it."

His answering nod is slow. I know him. I know that he's processing the information, letting it sink in. "This is so messed up," he mutters and scrubs his palm over his face. "She's *sixteen*."

"Yeah, and I lost my virginity at fifteen," I tell him.

"Don't remind me," he huffs. "I was jealous for weeks."

A smirk curls my lips and I can't resist asking, "Of me? Or of her?"

"Shut up," he snorts and headbutts my shoulder. Then he sighs. "A bit of both, I think."

"Yeah?"

"You're never letting go of my childhood crush on you, are you?"

"Not on your life."

***

The next morning is tense in the Durant household. Jay barely slept, tossing and turning all night, keeping me awake in turn. Not that my brain wasn't whirring all night on its own anyway. We're like the walking dead when we pull ourselves out of bed, a shared morning shower doing very little to wake either of us up. The fact that we don't even fool around under the warm spray is also telling of our moods.

We're in the kitchen, sipping at mugs of delicious, delicious caffeinated goodness when Mia tiptoes in cautiously, her eyes downcast and her bottom lip raw and swollen from being gnawed at.

She peeks up at us, giving me a flash of dark circles beneath reddened eyes, the blue of her irises popping against the red, then looks back at her feet, seemingly frozen.

"*Mimi,*" Jay infuses the softly spoken word with a thousand complex emotions, "sweetheart..."

She throws herself at him, sobbing before his arms have had time to wind around her back. There are words in there somewhere —apologies, mostly— and James just holds her and murmurs in her ear. I can't hear what he's saying, but I don't need to. He'll be reassuring her that he loves her, that he's there for her, that things will be okay.

He's been in her shoes. As much as his paternal urges to go and maim a teenage boy are railing inside him, he's a good dad who knows that the best thing he can do for her is support her. Besides, I told him about how terribly she's been beating herself up, and I don't think there's anything he could say to her that she hasn't already thought about herself. I imagine he knows what she's feeling more than I ever could, too.

"Do you want breakfast?" he asks her as she withdraws from the extended hug. He gestures towards me and grins. "Ev can make funny shape pancakes."

Instead of protesting that she's not a little kid anymore, the way she always does when we reference experiences from her younger years, she sniffles and nods. "With chocolate chips?"

I roll my eyes affectionately. "Is there any other way?"

We don't mention the elephant in the room as I make the batter, nor as I pour it into the frypan, nor as we sit down to eat the sugary treats.

However, I know Jay and Mia need to talk without me hanging around. Knowing that he'll confide in me later, I give his shoulder a squeeze after I've packed the breakfast plates into the dishwasher.

"I'm going to head into work for a bit," I tell him, explaining with my eyes that he should take the opportunity to actually talk to Mia. "Let me know if you need anything while I'm out."

It's the most domestic I've felt yet, and I barely stop myself from bending to press my lips to his in a quick kiss goodbye.

Jay reaches up and pats my hand on his shoulder. "Cheers," he says, licking his lips as if having the same thought I just did.

"You're being weird," Mia declares, and we both turn our heads to face her.

I casually remove my hand from James' shoulder as he says, "Forgive me if I don't know exactly how to act right now," in a tone that's both defensive and a little accusatory. I smack him upside the head.

"Stop it," I hiss at him, gesturing towards Mia. She's slumped forward in her chair, her expression crestfallen. "Remember how that felt, yeah?"

James swallows and nods, his own expression crumpling with regret. He sighs heavily and says, "I'm sorry, sweetheart. Let's go cuddle on the couch and talk, okay?"

"Text me if you need anything," I remind them both, then shoo them out of the kitchen and into the living room.

I grab my laptop bag, still unopened from where I dropped it on the kitchen bench yesterday, and sling it over my shoulder. I hesitate for a moment at the front door, my gaze lingering on the two most important people in my life —huddled together on the couch and murmuring in low voices— before I force myself to head outside and into my car.

***

I'm distracted all day. I can barely pay attention to the figures on my computer screen, the excel formulas —my favourite part of the job, and my pride and joy— all jumbling together and making no sense to me. I can't stop thinking about James and Mia. Whether he managed to keep his own panic aside to talk to her properly, and whether she opened up about the little douche-canoe she was dating (who, I should add, did not reply to any of her calls or texts yesterday) and about how she's been sneaking around behind our backs.

Yeah...she wasn't actually staying at Rose's place all those nights she said she was. A sixteen-year-old with her daddy's complete trust —even one as career-focused as Mia— is going to use that to her advantage. Who knew?

And the thing is, Jay and I have been too wrapped up in the excitement of our own relationship to notice.

God, I hope he doesn't feel as guilty about it as I do, but I have the feeling he will.

By two o'clock, I give up all pretence of working. I tell my boss I need to head off, and she waves me away blithely, and then I shoot off a quick text. If I don't talk about the thoughts eating me up inside, I'm going to scream.

Thankfully, a reply comes through within minutes, and I smile, tapping out my ETA of approximately twenty minutes.

***

"Come on in," Will Bradford says genially as he opens the front door of his apartment. He steps back and waves an arm, gesturing for me to accept the invitation. "Please ignore the mess. The boys were here and they like to wreak a bit of havoc wherever they go."

Despite his words, Will's smile stretches out his silvery stubble. It's obvious that he loves his grandsons —Jack's sons— and is more than happy to deal with the trail of blocks, legos and other toys that they leave behind in their wake.

I smile back at him and step carefully over the scattered toys, "Pretty sure your girl will be joining them soon, won't she?"

His and Connor's daughter, Victoria, is somewhere between one and two, from memory. I remember when Mia was that age; a little toddler terror. It's scary to think she may have one of her own soon enough, too.

"She already is," he answers, bending to pick up some of the mess. "Con's just changing her at the moment. He'll be out in a sec."

"Thanks," I bend to help him, ignoring his protests. "Sorry for just springing this on you guys." Technically, I sprung it on Connor, but his husband is a package deal, I guess, seeing as they live together and all. Jack lives in the apartment above them, actually, and again I wonder why I reached out to Con and not Jack, seeing as I've known Jack for longer.

"It's fine," Will responds, dropping his collection of blocks and stuff into the toy hamper in the middle of the room. I toss my handful in, too. He straightens up, rubbing at his back. "We're always happy to have friends drop by." Like Jack, Will has an American accent, and it's always a bit jarring to hear it when I've been surrounded by other Australians all day. He points at the couch. "Take a seat. Want anything to drink? Coffee? Tea? We might have a bottle of Coke in there…"

"Coffee would be great, actually." I sit on the grey couch and watch as he crosses the living room and then potters around in the adjoining kitchen.

"—and there's Daddy," Connor sing-songs as he leads a toddling little girl, dressed in pink overalls, through the living room and into the kitchen. The kid squeals and wobble-walks speedily to her other dad, pudgy fingers curling into the denim of his jeans once she slams into his legs.

Will scoops her up and settles her against his hip in a fluid, one-armed motion, wrapping up his coffee making efforts with his free arm. He smiles and chatters to his daughter as he goes about his business, explaining every step of what he's doing. "Let's press this button," he points to a button on Connor's fancy coffee machine, "and it will make your other daddy's coffee *just* the way he likes it." She smacks at the machine. Will presses the button for her, and she squeals and applauds clumsily as it whirrs to life, grinding beans and steaming milk. "Good job, princess!"

Connor kisses both his daughter and his husband on the cheek before taking the mug out from under the machine, replacing it with the next in line.

"Do you take sugar?" he asks, and it takes a second to realise that he's talking to me. I was too lost in their sweet domestic scene, wondering if Jay and I could have had something like that with Mia if we'd realised our feelings sooner.

If we could have something like that in a couple of years…

I clear my throat and give my head a shake, before smiling and accepting the outstretched mug. "Nah, just the milk's fine, thanks." Taking a moment to inhale the scent, I bring it to my mouth for a tentative sip, then sigh happily. Nothing beats a good coffee. "Perfect."

Connor chuckles and, after grabbing his own mug from the machine, folds himself into the chair across from me gracefully. "Now, I'm sure you didn't want to catch up just because you know I make the best coffees."

"*Ahem*," Will jokes as he wanders past us, Vicky still propped on his hip. "*Who* makes the best coffees?"

Connor rolls his eyes affectionately. "Our machine."

Will flips him off and I laugh at the exchange. It reminds me a little of me and Jay and the way we interact. Easy and sweet, with a little bit of banter.

"You don't mind if I take her over to visit with Toby and Vi?" Will asks after a beat. "I figured I'd put her in the pram and go for a walk. He'll be home from school by the time I get there." He looks over at me to explain, "He's a teacher. The walk from here is about half an hour, give or take. All downhill."

Connor grins. "I'll come pick you both up later. Plus, it will be nice to see Leo again. I miss having him upstairs."

"It won't be long before Jack begs him to move in again," Will answers, heading into the hallway which leads to the bedrooms and bathroom. I can hear cupboard doors opening and shutting as he continues with a raised voice, "only this time it'll be as his live-in boyfriend instead of his nanny."

"Yeah, I know," Connor agrees, then turns to me with a smirk, "we're taking bets on how long that takes. Want in?"

"Nah. I've got enough of that kind of melodrama in my life right now. I don't need to bet on someone else's."

Connor sits up straighter in his seat. "Oh? Does this have something to do with the gaudy ring you won't talk about?"

"Hey!" I splay my left hand over my chest dramatically. "That's my engagement ring you're mocking."

My timing is impeccable. Spluttering and coughing, Connor gasps for air over his coffee mug. He has dribbles of the light brown liquid down his chin and he swipes at them with the back of his hand. "You waited until I took a sip on purpose."

"You can't prove that."

He snorts. "Seriously, though. Engagement ring?" He cocks his head. "Your fiancé has...interesting taste in jewellery."

On game nights, we all shoot the shit and talk about our lives. I've mentioned going on dates with women a few times, but he gets points for not asking me outright whether I'm engaged to a woman or a man.

"I bought the rings as a joke, actually," I admit. "My best friend, James, he...got himself into a situation."

Connor raises his eyebrows and ignores his husband —who has bundled Vicky up in her pram with a nappy bag hung over the handles and has paused by the front door to bid us farewell— in preference of rolling his wrist in a 'hurry up' gesture.

I wave at Will somewhat apologetically. He just shakes his head, calls out a quick 'love you' to Connor, then leaves as I start telling my story.

"So, because it's Jay, I said that I'd pretend to be his fiancé. That...kind of snowballed." I give the summarised version of being roped into co-parenting for school events, and being forced to share beds and, ultimately, working out that I've fallen arse over teakettle for my best mate. "I had a little freak out about that. Not so much about being in love with a man, but being in love with my best friend. Turns out, he feels the same way about me, and we've spent a few weeks in a happy little relationship bubble."

"Why do I sense a 'but'?"

Pushing away the twelve-year-old-like instinct to laugh at the word 'butt', I nod. "Things are a bit...strained...in his house right now."

"The daughter?"

I nod. "Yeah. Mia." I smile softly. "I love that kid."

"Did she not take the news of you being together well?"

"She doesn't know yet. We were going to tell her —we actually had a conversation about that the other day, after Jay came out to his colleague— but she dropped a pretty big bomb of her own."

Placing his mug on the coffee table, Connor inclines his head again. He reminds me a little of a chihuahua every time he does. I'm not quite sure why. Maybe it's the big, round, curious eyes.

Exhaling, I tell him, "She might be pregnant. And, you know, Jay was a teen dad himself, so he's...well, he's kind of alternating between freaking out and wanting to be the kind of parent to her that his were for him. The difference is, she's still in high school while he was already at uni...so, yeah. Things are...tense. And I might have made them worse."

He blinks. "How?"

"I, uh, I told Jay that if she was putting the baby up for adoption...maybe" —I clear my throat and look at the remnants of coffee and milk foam swirling at the bottom of my mug— "maybe we could adopt it."

"*Jesus*," he breathes. "That's..."

"I know."

"It's just—"

"No, I get it. We've only been dating —really dating— for, like, a month. And kids are a lifetime commitment, and they put strain on any relationships, let alone new relationships, and...I just thought, y'know, that kid would be a quarter James."

"So," Connor says tentatively, as if he's trying to be as tactful and gentle as possible, "did you make that suggestion because you want kids? Or because some part of you feels like, with James as its biological grandfather—what?"

My face must be contorted in the same level of rising horror that I can feel. "Grandfather," I repeat. "Holy shit. He...he might be a granddad at thirty-five."

Connor's lips twitch in amusement before he schools his expression. "That's generally what happens when someone's kid has a kid."

"Would...would that make it weird? Adopting his grandkid and raising it as his own?"

"I'm raising my niece as my daughter, so you're asking the wrong person," he shrugs. "But, for the record, no. I don't think that's weird. However..."

I sigh. "You're going back to asking if it's an obligation thing, aren't you?"

"Is it?"

"You'd make an excellent therapist, you know that?"

"Evan..."

"I don't know. And, you know, it's all hypothetical right now. Like, there's a fifty-fifty chance that she's not pregnant because she took three tests and they were inconclusive, so we're waiting on blood test results and this could all be a moot point anyway."

Connor nods and he sits back into his seat. "But maybe you freaked yourself out by making that suggestion to James to begin with? Is that what's bothering you? Because it sounds like everything got serious really quickly and maybe your brain is starting to catch up on how many huge changes you've made in such a short amount of time?"

As he says it, I start to relax, feeling *seen*. "Yeah," I swallow. "Yeah. I think...I think that's it. Like...I know Jay is my person. He's *it* for me. That feels right. But even that is huge because he is a guy, and he's my best friend, and we're going to have to tell our families and stuff at some point, and they'll all want to know why it took us so long to work it out. And, yeah, I've kind of been a stepdad all year, and now even that seems to have gotten crazy serious all of a sudden. Not that it wasn't serious before, because looking after kids is always serious, but..."

Jesus Christ, I even ramble like Jay now.

"It's a lot," Connor acknowledges. "And maybe telling Jay that you would raise his hypothetical grandkid with him was the straw that broke the camel's back."

"So...what do I do?"

"Talk to Jay. Maybe talk to an actual counsellor or therapist. These are *huge* life-changing issues and it's okay to get help working through them."

I consider that for a moment. I do feel lighter after sharing it all with him. Maybe breaking it down and talking to a professional isn't a bad idea. Jay might even benefit from it, too.

"In fact," Connor says, as if reading my mind, "no matter what happens with Mia, you should probably all consider it anyway."

I think about the secrets Mia has been keeping from us and, in turn, the one we've been keeping from her and I find myself nodding again. "You're not wrong."

Chapter Seventeen

James

"I'm not mad that you're having sex," the words are awkward as they leave my mouth, and I cringe just as much as Mia does. "But I am…I don't know…sad, I guess, that you didn't even tell us…uh…me that you were dating anyone. That you…that you felt like you needed to lie and sneak around…"

Like I have been with Ev.

Guilt prickles up the back of my neck and my stomach churns.

I haven't actually been lying to her, though, have I? I had every intention of telling her about Ev and me. I did. I even told him so on Tuesday. Fuck, that feels like forever ago, despite today being only Friday.

Mia bites her bottom lip and looks away with a despondent shrug. "It was just dating. Nothing serious."

"Nothing—" I cut off my high-pitched, incredulous echo with a snap of my jaws together. I try to push down the frustrated anger, to see things from her perspective. "Sweetheart," I manage to bring my tone back down to something softer, more understanding, "sex is always serious."

She scoffs. "So you're serious with all your Tinder dates?"

"I don't sleep with all...No. No, you know what? I've taken every single sexual encounter in my life seriously, Mia."

"I didn't say I wasn't taking sex seriously," she snaps back at me. "But I was just dating him. I wasn't...It was just supposed to be a high school fling. I wasn't, like, planning marriage or..." she trails off, cringing again.

"Or kids?"

Damn it. That came out too harsh, too.

"It's not like you planned me."

Ouch. True, but...ouch.

"Mia..."

"Did you hate me? Resent me? Because I *will* resent this kid...if there is a kid. It's not...it's not *fair.*"

My heart hurts. All through her childhood, anytime she's been hurting, I've felt it. I've always taken on her pain in my own way, feeling guilty for not being able to prevent the skinned knees or broken bones or whatever viral illnesses she picked up at school. I know I couldn't have stopped any of it, just like I really can't stop her from feeling future pain, physically or emotionally.

"No, sweetheart," I answer her through a throat thickened by empathetic tears, "but I chose you. I chose to raise you by myself. If...if there *is* a choice to be made, you don't have to make the same choice I did."

"Really? You wouldn't judge me if..."

"Not a chance." Whatever frustration I was feeling has melted away and I pull her in for another hug. "I've got your back, Mimi. No matter what you choose to do. Every single option has its pros and cons. None of them are easy, and nobody but you can decide which choice is the right choice for you right now."

"A-and if I kept it? If...if I had to leave Winchester and go back to a normal high school...you wouldn't hate me for wasting all that money?"

"I wouldn't ever hate you for anything. And it's not a waste. Even if we pull you out of that school first thing Monday morning, you've still had six months of advanced drama classes and experience that you wouldn't have had at your old school. That's still worth it."

She flings her arms around me for the umpteenth time today and buries her face in the crook of my neck. "I'm sorry, Dad."

I go to tell her that the only thing she should be sorry for is lying to me, but I can't even bring myself to do that. "There's nothing to be sorry for, Mimi. You're growing up, and sometimes life stuff like this happens, even when you're being careful."

"...and if I wasn't?"

I close my eyes and sigh. Eighteen-year-old me wasn't always careful, either. "You're only human."

"You're the best, Dad." It's not said with her usual cheek. It's spoken softly and with so many levels of emotion that I want to cry. Maybe later, when I don't have to be strong for her, I'll let go.

"Just remember," I tell her, trying to cheer us both up even though things are going to be strained until we know exactly what the next steps need to be, "when you're receiving your first Logie or, better yet, your first Oscar, *I'm* the first person you thank in that acceptance speech. None of this 'I want to thank the Academy' crap."

Her laughter, however short and weak and watery it might be, is like music to my ears. "You're such a dork."

"Yeah," I agree, "but you love me."

***

When Ev lets himself in in the early hours of the evening, he finds me and Mia pretty much exactly where he left us, only there's a spread of takeaway Thai food on the coffee table and we're watching *Mean Girls* together on the big screen TV I splurged on last Christmas.

There's a longing in his gaze and I know it's because he wants to bend down and kiss my lips. I wish that he could as well, but now doesn't seem like the right moment to announce our relationship. Not with the stress of everything else going on.

Instead of giving in to temptation, he drops down on Mia's other side and reaches for the container of Penang curry, picking up the clean fork we grabbed with him in mind. He gives Mia a little nudge and a warm smile before digging in to his meal, not at all bothered that we obviously ate an early dinner before he got home.

"So," he says right as Kady is breaking up pieces of her crown on the screen, "I was thinking that maybe we should, uh, think about therapy, or something?"

"Why?" Mia asks, only for Ev to raise both his eyebrows.

"Really?" he asks, sounding mildly incredulous. "You're not, like, completely traumatised by...everything?"

She gives me a look that asks 'is he for real?' before turning back to Ev. "I mean...not any more than you'd expect?" She reaches out and pats my knee. "Dad and I had a long, emotional talk about it all and we're good. I'm good. I mean, I'm still scared, but...I'm okay. As okay as I can be until I know one way or the other. So, yeah, maybe I'm in limbo? But...it's okay."

Ev chews on his mouthful of food, his eyebrows drawing together. He's wearing his glasses again and, coupled with his serious expression, he looks sexy as fuck.

Focus, James.

"What about the sneaking around and the not telling the whole truth about where you were going? You don't think we need to maybe talk to someone about why you did that?"

Mia sits up a little straighter, frowning to match Ev's expression. "No offence, Evvy," she says, and I brace myself for impact because any time a teenaged girl says 'no offence', she *definitely* means 'take *all* the offence', "but you're *not* my parent. You're not even really my stepparent. You're just faking it. You're *just* my godfather and that's...well, that's just a title, isn't it?"

Ev looks crushed. Then he turns his soulful dark eyes on me. "Are we just faking it, Jay?"

Oh boy, that's a loaded question.

The answer should be easy. No. Nothing about my feelings are fake. Nothing about our relationship is fake. But the fact that we've kept it from Mia because *I* was too scared to say anything earlier...

"No." I can't be that scared little boy anymore. And after everything I said to Mia about sneaking around, I can't continue to be a hypocrite, either.

Maybe Ev's right. Maybe we should get some counselling.

Mia twists her neck to face me again. "What?" She frowns at me, then looks back at Ev, then back at me again. "What does that mean?"

"I..." I start, but struggle to find the words at first. "Ev and I..."

Her eyes, so much like mine, widen and her jaw drops. "Wait..."

"We were going to tell you. Today, actually," I fish my phone from my pocket, wanting to prove it to her, but she's shaking her head and pushing to her feet, moving to pace in front of the TV like a caged animal.

Her accusatory index finger swishes in the air, directed at Ev, then me, then Ev. "You two are...?"

"Dating?" I suggest.

"In love?" Ev says at the same time.

My heart thumps in my chest.

"*In love?*" Mia sounds mildly hysterical. She flings her hands into the air, every bit the dramatic sixteen-year-old girl. "How long has this been going on?"

"All our lives?" Ev answers, equally dramatic.

I glare at him. "That's not—*no*. You know that's not what she meant." I look to Mia, pleading for her to understand. "It's, uh, it's been official for about a month," I tell her.

Being the smart girl she is, she narrows her gaze. "And before that? It was *unofficial* for how long?"

"I don't think that's any—" Ev starts defensively, and I cut him off.

"A couple of months." The look I send him is equal parts apology and daring him to argue with me for finally being honest with her. He sits back and shuts his pretty mouth. I turn to Mia again. "I was...confused, Mia. And scared of admitting my feelings for him. And...and afraid that telling you would change things. Between you and me, I mean. And that was wrong of me, I know. It hurt him, and it's upsetting you, and it was unfair on me, too. And that's all on me, okay? I know it is."

"Baby..." Ev reaches for me and Mia makes a strangled sound.

"That's...that's so *weird*," she declares. Then, as if hearing herself, rushes to add, "Not...not that you're bi. Or gay? Or...no. Not that. Just...you guys aren't like that with each other. You don't *do* pet names and stuff. You're not...you're best friends, not..." she waves her hand over us, where we've given up the pretence and Ev has settled in at my side, his arm wrapped around me. "Whatever the hell this is."

"In love," Ev repeats himself, gentler this time. Affectionate. "I love your dad, Mimi. Always have. But, yeah, the feeling is more romantic now, I guess. Best friends with—"

"Oh, god, don't say benefits," she covers her face with her hands.

Ev snorts. "I was going to say romance on the side, actually." Then, because he's still a shit-stirrer, says, "We have you to thank for this, really. If you hadn't come up with the fake engagement thing, we probably never would've realised how we felt about each other."

"This is insane," Mia murmurs towards the ceiling. Then she looks at me. "How do you go your entire adult life without knowing you're into your best friend?"

"Oh," Ev grins as he rushes to answer her, speaking over the top of my protests, "he admitted he had a crush on me when we were kids. But I was oblivious, and he still liked girls, so apparently he just pretended it wasn't a thing and that was that." He shakes his head and leans forward, as if delivering a secret that I can't hear. "Your dad's a bit of an idiot, really."

"You're both idiots," she declares and then sits down heavily on the armchair positioned sideways to the couch. "Seriously. What the actual fuck?"

"Language," I scold, but Ev laughs.

"Yeah, well, I feel a bit dumb for taking all this time to cotton on," he tells her easily. "We've always been closer and more touchy-feely than most best mates. I just figured it was 'cause we're enlightened and comfortable within ourselves. But I guess it was more that we were always meant to be together."

She makes an exaggerated gagging sound. "That is disgustingly sweet."

"It is, isn't it?" Ev sounds a little too proud of that fact.

I clear my throat and hold out my hand, palm facing upwards. "Forgive me, sweetheart," I all but beg, "I should have said something sooner. Of all people, we shouldn't have kept it from you for as long as we did. I just...coming out is...well, it's confronting. I'm in my mid-thirties. Shouldn't I have known myself better than this?" Ev tenses and I shake my head. "Don't answer that. I just...I'm sorry, Mimi. We should have told you weeks ago."

For a moment, I'm almost afraid that she's going to reject my apology, but she rolls her eyes and takes my hand, squeezing it tightly. "You're still an idiot," she says, and her lips twitch, "but you've got my back no matter what, and I've got yours, too."

The urge to cry hits me all over again.

This time, I give in to it.

Chapter Eighteen

Evan

Mia asks both me and Jay to accompany her to her follow-up doctor's appointment on Monday. As far as I'm aware, she spent the bulk of the weekend writing up pros and cons lists for her options under the 'worst case' scenario of the blood tests changing her life forever. Mia has always been a planner. She's always had an ace up her sleeve.

This is the one time where she hasn't been prepared and I think that has been the cause of most of her stress. Well, that and the whole 'possibly pregnant at sixteen' thing.

We get a few raised eyebrows when all three of us stand up when her name is called, but we don't pay them any mind. We're more concerned about Mia.

Doctor Rogers greets Jay with the familiarity of someone who has been their family's medical practitioner for years before she turns to me and offers me a much warmer smile than she did the first time we met. I just nod and then she turns her full attention to the teenager gripping both our hands for dear life.

"Okay, well, let's not prolong the suspense," Doctor Rogers says as she pulls up the blood test results on her screen. She glances at them, nods, then looks Mia in the eye and informs her, "You're *not* pregnant."

Jay slumps with relief as Mia actually whoops for joy, and I...can't actually pinpoint how I feel. Glad that things are *not* as scary and stressful as they could be for Mia, but also maybe a tiny bit...disappointed? Deflated?

I can't quite understand why.

It's not like I wanted my sixteen-year-old goddaughter to be pregnant.

But after all the build up of tension and stress and strategizing for worst case scenarios, this feels mildly anticlimactic.

"You should also be happy to hear that your results came back negative for sexually transmitted infections as well," Doctor Rogers continues, "though I do hope you will consider using condoms going forward."

Mia's cheeks turn bright red, but she nods. "Yes. Of course. But, honestly, I think this has scared me off sex for a while."

I'm pretty sure Jay's relieved to hear that, too, but he's smart enough not to say anything. Doctor Rogers strikes me as the kind of woman who wouldn't hesitate to tell him where he could shove any thoughts of policing his daughter's bodily autonomy. She's scary, but all sorts of awesome.

"I'm going to refer you to a colleague of mine," she tells Mia, typing away at her computer, "because experiences like these can definitely shake your confidence and, sometimes, as supportive as family can be, it's easier to talk to an unbiased party."

I can't help but feel a little vindicated that the doctor is making the same suggestion of therapy. I squeeze Mia's hand and bump my shoulder into hers, creating a knock-on effect into her dad.

"I told you so," I sing-song under my breath.

"And," the doctor continues, looking over at me pointedly before smiling at Jay, "I'd suggest you and…?"

"Evan," I remind her easily.

"Evan," she nods, "might also benefit with a session or two, just to deal with any lingering fear or resentment or," she shoots an apologetic look at Mia, "distrust which might have arisen over the course of the past few days."

I bob my head. I want to tell her that I already suggested it, but there's no point.

I do, however, plan on serenading my boyfriend and his daughter with the strains of my 'I told you so' song for the entire drive back to their house.

As if sensing my plan to be smug and rub it in, Jay sighs and says, "Yes, honey, I *know*. You were right. We were wrong."

"Well, that takes all the fun out of my I-told-you-so-ing," I pout dramatically.

"Oh, God," Mia complains between us, "I liked it better when you were oblivious BFFs. This is just painful to watch."

"I thought you loved having me around as your stepdad," I tease. "It was all your idea to begin with, remember?"

"You're never going to let me forget that, are you?"

"Nope," I pop the 'p', grinning from ear-to-ear, my weird moment from earlier all but forgotten. "You're the reason we got together."

She looks at the doctor, who seems thoroughly confused by our entire production. "Kill me now."

Being the intelligent woman that she is, Miranda Rogers claps her hands together and says, "Well, unless there's anything else concerning you medically, you're all free to go." She hands Jay the referrals she just printed out. "Be sure to arrange at least one appointment for her, James. Being sixteen is hard enough, you know?"

He nods. "Thanks Miranda."

Then we're finally leaving the clinic and we feel like an entirely different group than the one that filtered in earlier. Mia is carefree and laughing, James is smiling, and I...am about to get hit by a car.

Well, I think in the split second before the collision, shoving Mia and James back onto the footpath behind me, before the squeal of tyres and sudden searing pain has a chance to register, *I didn't have this on my bingo card for today.*

Chapter Nineteen

James

"He's still in surgery," Ev's mum, Janet, tells me as she takes the stiff plastic seat at my side. "Dennis has gone to get us some coffee. The good stuff, if he can find it. Not the swill they pedal in the machines here."

I just nod, still feeling numb from the shock of the accident. I don't know how Ev saw that car come flying around the corner, but he saved me and Mia without a thought for himself.

If I'd thought seeing Mia distraught over possibly being pregnant was hard, watching her scream and weep over Ev's unconscious form was ten times worse.

I'd take a hundred yesterdays over today.

Even worse than that, though, was not being able to ride in the ambulance with him, because only one of us could have gone and I couldn't leave Mia behind. It was getting to the hospital after a white-knuckled, whirlwind of a drive, only to be told that I'm not listed as his next of kin. His parents are.

No amount of telling them that I'm his spouse made any difference.

Mia and I just had to sit and wait.

And wait.

And wait.

It was agonising.

Janet and Dennis turned up an hour or so later. They were taken away to talk to doctors, and when they returned, we all got taken into a more secluded waiting room for families of emergency patients.

And we've been waiting ever since. I've lost track of the hours now, and I can't bring myself to pull out my phone to check the time. Not when my lock screen has a photo of me, Ev, and Mia taken at her leadership camp. The camp that changed my life. Changed both our lives.

Mia's asleep next to me, her head cushioned on my shoulder, a tiny trickle of drool creating a wet spot. She'll be mortified when she wakes up. Ev would tease her mercilessly for it.

My heart pangs again.

Then I remember that Janet said something and I blink, giving my head a minute shake, careful not to wake Mia. "Sorry, what?"

"He's still in surgery, but they don't think the knock to the head has caused any damage there," she tells me, twisting her hands in her lap. "Just...something to do with his, um, his spleen and something about his ribs? I couldn't follow it all. Just that they were more concerned with where the bull bar impacted him than when he hit his head when he landed, but" —she chokes on a sob, bringing a trembling, age-spotting hand to her mouth— "th-they're watching for swelling and bleeding just in case."

I want to hug her, my second mother, whose house I spent just as much time in as my own during my childhood, but I can't move. Not just because of Mia, either, but because I'm paralysed by fear.

I think back to Thursday night, to him telling me that I'm his person, that he would raise a hypothetical baby with me, and my terror that the stress of doing so would tear us apart. Now I'm afraid that I'll lose him anyway, and I want to go back in time and shake myself for not responding differently. Not telling him how much I appreciated the thought he had put in to our potential future. Not thanking him for loving and caring for my daughter as much as I do. For loving me so much that he would settle down so completely like that.

I don't realise I'm crying until Janet's hand cups my cheek, her thumb swiping away my tears. "Oh, James," she sniffles, "I know."

Suddenly, I can't stand the fact that she doesn't really know. Yes, she knows I love Ev as my best friend. She might even think that I love him like a brother...but that thought sours my gut, making me feel ill.

It's the furthest from brotherly love that we can get at this point.

At the same time, I can't possibly out her son to her. I'm sure Ev would understand if I told his parents, he'd want me to be able to lean on them while he fights for his life in surgery, but...I just can't do it.

And then *my* mother is walking through the door, followed by Ev's dad, Dennis, and my own. It makes sense that Jan or Dennis would have called them. Our families have always been close, and if I look at Ev's parents as my surrogate family, I know he sees mine the same way.

My parents are a decade younger than Ev's, seeing as he was Jan's miracle baby, arriving when she and Dennis were in their early forties, but right now their worry makes them look just as old as their friends. It shouldn't comfort me to see them so upset, but on some strange level it does. They adore Ev as much as I do. I'm not alone in my worry and grief.

"Mum," I suddenly feel like a lost kid instead of an adult in his mid-thirties. I want to be wrapped in her arms and told that everything's going to be okay.

Mia stirs and lifts her head, staring blearily at her grandmother before she's up and launching herself into my mum's arms. I don't begrudge her that. My mum gives amazing hugs.

Mum tucks Mia into her left side and gestures for me to join at her right, and I go willingly, falling into the group embrace almost desperately. I take strength from the hug, bolstered by Mum's lips to my temple and her whispered, "He'll be okay."

"I love him," I blurt, hiding my ugly tears in the crook of her neck.

"I know," she says, and I feel Dad's hand clasp my shoulder and squeeze his own reassurance.

"No, Mum," I pull back, looking her in the eye, pleading with her to understand, "I *love* him."

Her smile is soft and sympathetic. Knowing. "Darling," she chuckles wetly, "we've known that since you were fifteen."

I don't even have the energy to be confused or flabbergasted. "Oh." I clear my throat and look around, finding Jan and Dennis nodding as well. My cheeks heat. Despite my resolve not to out him, I wipe my eyes and say, "We're together now. It's...it's new. We were going to tell everyone but...it's been a hectic week."

"Damn it," Dennis sighs and pulls out his wallet, handing a crisp fifty dollar note over to my dad. "You couldn't have held out another eighteen months? *Oi.*" He rubs at his side, where his wife has elbowed him.

I blink at the exchange. "You...you were betting on...what, exactly?"

"When you two would get your heads out of your arses and see what was right in front of you," Dennis answers with a shrug. "My money was on Mia's graduation."

Despite the situation, Mia starts to giggle. "Evvy's going to find that hilarious," she explains when I turn my bewildered stare on her, still tucked into her grandmother's side.

They look very alike, seeing as I take after my mum and Mia takes after me. All blonde hair and blue eyes, with the same straight nose and angular jawlines. The older Mia gets, the more she reminds me of my mother, and it's startling to see them side-by-side after a few months without seeing each other in person.

Where has the year gone?

It's been a whirlwind of school events and work and focusing on our (apparently-not-so-surprising) romantic relationship. I've spoken to my parents, sure, but we haven't seen each other enough. I feel guilty about that, especially when their support remains so unwavering.

In the face of Mia's continued giggles, I can't help but smile and chuckle a little, however weakly. "Wouldn't surprise me if he was in on it."

"Nah," she shakes her head, "he can't keep secrets from you."

That's true. I flash back to that night a couple of months ago, when he'd worked out that he had feelings for me and *had* to tell me immediately, and my heart clenches. He's always been the brave one. The one unafraid to be completely honest and upfront.

I could learn from him. Be brave for him.

With our combined families' obvious support, I know I can be.

Now I just need him to make it through surgery.

Chapter Twenty

Evan

Everything fucking hurts.

Everything.

My stomach. My chest. Even my freaking eyelids.

What the hell happened?

I blink, squinting against lights that are *far* too bright, and I whine through a throat that is scratchy and sore.

Am I sick?

I don't remember getting sick.

"Hang on, love," a familiar voice says, and I feel a gentle touch to my hand as she says, "Den, can you hit the lights?" Then the voice —my mum's voice— says, "Don't try to talk yet. You were intubated. Have a couple sips of water. *Just* sips." I feel a straw pressed to my lips. One of those awful paper ones that I hate. But I *am* thirsty, so I sip and wince as I swallow. "That's it," she says gently. "Good."

"Wha—?" I start, and my voice sounds weird to my own ears. Groggy and strained.

"You're in the hospital, love."

Hospital?

Still squinting, and feeling dizzy and disoriented, I ask, "Why?"

Mum *tsks*. "You don't remember?"

I'd tell her I wouldn't ask if I did, but that would take up too much energy. I manage a mumbled, "Nup."

"There was an accident. You got hit by a car."

I...what?!

"James said it came out of nowhere. You were just stepping off the footpath at the doctor's."

James...

"You chose a pretty good place to get into an accident, at least," Dad's voice pipes up from the other side of what has to be my hospital bed.

"That's not funny, Den," Mum scolds him.

If I had the energy, I'd laugh, because it did appeal to my lame sense of humour. Dad's where I get it from.

"Ev thinks it is," he defends himself, "don't you, bud?"

"Uh huh," I force the answer out as my struggling eyelids get heavier.

Mum pats my hand again. I know it's her, because the touch is soft. Plus it's on the same side of the bed as her voice. "The nurse said you'll sleep a bit, yet. It's okay. We'll all be here when you wake up again."

"J'mes?" I ask, because I haven't heard his voice yet and I need to.

"He took Mia home," Mum explains. "He'll be back soon, love. Just rest."

I give in to the heaviness of my eyelids and drift off.

When I wake up again, there's less pain and my head feels less foggy. There's also a big, warm hand closed over mine, and I squeeze it the second I realise that it's Jay.

"Hey," he sounds relieved and tired.

I slowly open my eyes and he comes into focus as I adjust to the light. "Hey," I greet him back. I want to reach out and cup his face, but my limbs feel heavy.

I close my eyes as he cards fingers through my hair. "How are you feeling?"

"Sore." I frown, vague memories of talking to my mum filtering back to me. "Was I...was there a car?"

Jay's handsome face falls and he nods. "Guy came flying around the corner just as we were leaving the doctor's. You'd already stepped out to cross into the carpark. You shoved Mia and me back, but you didn't have time to get out of the way. He saw you too late. Slammed on the brakes, but..." his voice is thick with emotion. "It was awful, Ev. You were in surgery for hours. I thought..."

"It's gonna take more than some idiot who can't follow road rules to get rid of me, baby," I tell him, and he swallows hard.

"I love you," he says, then he looks down and mumbles, "I told our parents about us."

Warmth spreads through me. "Yeah?" He nods. A smile curls my lips. "I'm so proud of you, Jay."

The blue of his eyes pops against the red rims and dark circles underneath them as he looks back up at me. "You are? Even if I outed you to our parents? All of them?"

I chuckle and then wince at the pain that blossoms in my abdomen and chest. "Yeah, babe. All of them. How'd they take it?"

"They had a bet going," he answers distractedly, frowning. "You're in pain," he fusses, pressing the call button for the nurse before I can stop him. Then he grasps my hands again and squeezes. "Move in with me."

"I don't need more pain meds," I insist. "They make me sleepy. And...what? Move in? Baby..."

"I almost lost you," he explains, sounding as wrecked as he looks. "I know it's fast, but...this just made me realise how much I need you." He gives me emotional whiplash when he follows that up with, "You do need the meds. Sleep helps your body heal."

"I'm fine," I start to push myself into a seated position without the aid of the bed's remote. I immediately regret it as pain lances through me, and I groan.

Yeah, okay, that was a mistake.

Nevertheless, he's just dropped a pretty huge, life-changing bomb on me and we can't pretend he hasn't. "Jay, baby, I can't move in with you. It's too fast, and you're only asking as a knee-jerk reaction to the accident."

His face falls. "But..."

"I'm not saying never. I'm not even saying not soon. But now isn't a great time to make huge life decisions like that." I pout at him. "And now you've got me having to be the rational one. I don't like it, Jay." I try to sit up again and groan again as I remember why I stopped trying a few moments ago. I hate that I can't hold him and promise him that, even though I'm turning him down, I'm still not going anywhere.

"Stay down," he insists. "You're in pain. The meds will help."

"I don't want meds. We need to talk about this."

Then the arsehole pulls out the big guns just as the nurse walks in. "Look; accept the pain meds, and when you wake up Mia will be here, too. She's been worried sick about you. We all have."

Taking a deep breath, the weight of the situation settles over me. If our situations were reversed, I'd be beside myself, and I'd probably be begging him to never leave my sight again, too.

"I'm sorry for scaring you all." Not that any of it was actually my fault, mind you. But...I can't think of anything better to say to express myself right now. Blame the fact that I was hit by a freaking car however many hours ago.

James shakes his head, his grip on my hand tightening. "Don't apologize. Just focus on your recovery. We need you, Ev." He swallows again, and his eyes look suspiciously moist. "*I* need you."

I close my eyes for a moment, letting the exhaustion wash over me. "You're playing dirty," I accuse him, but then I sigh. "I need you too, you know. I love you."

"Always," James replies, his voice filled with emotion. Then he straightens up and sniffs, levelling a weak glare at me. "But if you ever pull a stunt like yesterday again..."

I manage a small smile at his attempt at levity. "I know. You'll kill me yourself."

"And don't you forget it."

***

"You owe me fifty bucks, bud," Dad declares when he and Mum walk into my hospital room.

I'm sitting up this time, propped up by the magical adjustable hospital bed, slowly eating the surprisingly not-too-shabby chicken korma I ordered through the hospital's room service system.

Yep. You heard me correctly. Room service. In a hospital. And it's not bland slop. Boy, how times have changed since I broke my arm as a kid.

With my fork halfway to my mouth, I frown at him. "For...parking? That seems a little stinge, Dad, even for you. Need I remind you I got hit by a bus—"

"A car," James lifts his gaze from his work laptop to correct me.

"A *huge* car," I embellish, just to stir him, "only yesterday?"

Dad rolls his eyes and looks at my boyfriend. "You sure you want to be stuck with him? You can do better, James."

"Hey," I complain, but secretly I'm *buzzing* inside.

I've introduced my parents to girlfriends over the years, but they've never treated any of them like they were part of the family. Maybe because they knew I wasn't serious about them, or because they didn't know them well enough (which is on me).

But Jay is already part of the family, and their acceptance of this change in our relationship, while not at all unexpected, makes me incredibly thankful that my parents are such great people.

"Why do I owe you money?" I ask again.

"I lost a bet because of you." Dad sulks, but his eyes are twinkling. He points his index finger at me. "Couldn't keep it in your pants for another eighteen months, could you?"

Mum moans and covers her face. "Den, seriously?"

I look at Jay. "What the hell?"

"I guess you were still a little out of it earlier," he replies and shuts his laptop, giving me his undivided attention. Beside him, Mia looks up from her phone and smirks.

"Grandpa and Uncle Den had a bet about when you two would finally realise you were in *lurve*," she drags the word out, making a face. "Still ew, by the way. 'Cause you're old."

I point at her. "The other day you said it was because we're best mates."

"Either way," she shrugs, "ew."

"Anyway," Jay redirects the conversation, waving his hand vaguely over his daughter's form, curled into the visitor's chair, fingers tapping away on her phone screen, "pretty much what she said. Our parents apparently had our feelings figured out before we did. They gambled on when we'd finally work it out. Dad won."

"By eighteen months," my dad grumbles, but there's no heat behind it. "You made it all this time, why not another year and a bit?"

"Half, Dad," I get playfully condescending, "year and a half."

He flips me off. Mum sighs dramatically, but then she winks at me. "I can see you're feeling better, love. How's the pain?"

"Manageable." I *might* have fought the nurse on the last dosage she planned on giving me. I didn't want to be so drowsy anymore. "And I'm eating. See?" I lift my fork and finally slide the mouthful of curry between my lips. It's lukewarm now, but still tasty enough. "So," I add after I've swallowed, "they should be letting me out soon, yeah?"

"When you can walk and go to the toilet on your own, yeah," Jay nods, and I scowl.

"I want to go home *now*."

"Geez, you weren't even this bad when you were eight." Dad says. He looks at James again. "Seriously, nobody will judge you if you change your mind about him." He hisses as Mum slaps his chest, and he rubs at the sore spot with a pout. "I was only joking."

"Idiot," she mutters. Then she pats my foot, which is covered by the hospital issued white waffle blanket. "You'll be out in no time. James has called your work and explained the situation, and they're not expecting you to come back for a couple of weeks at least."

"Thanks, baby," I tell him, delighting in the way his cheeks turn pink at the pet name.

On his other side, Mia gags exaggeratedly.

"Get used to it," Jay nudges her.

"Only eighteen more months and I'll be at uni," she responds under her breath. "I'll think of it like a prison sentence."

"So dramatic," I tease. Then I smile widely at Jay. "She *does* take after me, after all."

Mia rolls her eyes, but I can tell that she's trying not to smile.

I love that kid.

In fact, I think as I look around the room, *I love everyone.*

At first I think I'm just lucky, but then I glance over my shoulder and notice the nurse pumping a new dose of painkillers into my IV.

Or maybe, I muse, *I'm just high.*

Chapter Twenty-One

James

"**W**here's Mister B, Mister D?" Joey asks, leaning over the canteen's front counter. He doesn't seem to care that there are a bunch of hungry, impatient teenagers behind him. He twists his head from side to side, looking for my boyfriend. Instead, he finds the big, tattooed guy Ev sent in his place. Jack. His eyes widen. "And who's the new hottie?"

"*Joey*," I say warningly. It's been two weeks since Ev's accident, and while he's back on his feet (and practically moved into my house because I refused to let him out of my sight for longer than necessary), he still tires easily and can't lift anything heavy, so he called in a favour with one of his soccer friends.

(I haven't heard the end of his 'I miss soccer' whinging, either.)

"You didn't break up, did you?" the kid's gaze flits to my ring and something that looks a lot like relief flashes over his face.

"No," I tell him, "we're still very happy. He just...had surgery a little while ago and he's recovering. His friend, Jack, is here instead."

Joey nods, then leans all the way over the bench to check the firefighter out. "Is Jack single?"

"Jack is not. He's also twice your age." I gently push him back onto his side of the counter. "Now, are you ordering, or just holding up the line behind you?"

"Does Jack like men?" he tries again, batting his lashes in Jack's direction.

"Alright, that's it," I point to the exit lane. "Shoo."

He pouts, but he leaves, and Jack snorts. "Kids are super ballsy now, aren't they?"

"He's got an accent?!" Joey pops his head in through the back door to the canteen.

Sophie, one half of the other couple rostered on today, laughs and then chases him away.

"He's a menace," I say, but it's fond.

The kid has grown on me, too, it turns out.

After lunch time is over and we've cleaned and sterilised the canteen, Jack and I walk back down to the school carpark. He seems like a nice guy, and we've been bonding over his experiences as a relatively new fulltime dad to twin four-year-olds.

"Uh, Mister D?" I just about jump out of my skin as Joey pushes off the bonnet of my car, where he was obviously waiting for us.

"Shouldn't you be in class?"

"Yeah, but, um, I just...I just wanted to make sure Mister B is really okay."

I nod. "That's sweet. He's fine, I promise. He's actually really whiny because he wants to be back out playing soccer again, but his doctor won't let him yet." I cock my head. "You really should be getting back to class."

Joey nods and sighs. "Yeah."

"Is everything okay?" I look the kid over. He doesn't seem his usual bouncy self, but a lot of kids start hitting the wall in the second half of the school year. "Did you want to talk to Ev about something specific?"

"Yeah, no, I'm fine. I just...I like Mister B a lot. And you," he hurries to add, as if I'm going to be offended that he likes Evan more than me. "But, yeah...I just...I've missed seeing you guys at stuff."

I remember what he's said in the past, about not knowing many other same-sex couples and, now that I've started to go through the coming out process, I think I get it more. He doesn't feel like he fits in, especially when he's not getting acceptance at home, and he feels safe with Ev and, to some extent, with me. A kinship, if you will.

"Why don't you see if Mia feels up for hosting a drama club slumber party at our place?" I ask him, giving him an excuse to hang out with likeminded people without being weird about it. "Tell her that her dads will buy all the hipster gluten-free vegan pizzas your hearts desire."

His eyes light up and he bounces on the balls of his feet. "Yeah?"

"Yeah," I nod. "Now get back to class before your warden —I mean, principal— finds you out without a hall pass or whatever they call them these days."

"You're the best, Mister D," he tells me, and I watch as he heads off up the hedge-lined path to the main area of the school.

When I turn back around, Jack is smirking at me, tattooed arms folded over his big, broad chest. "What?" I ask him.

"That was nice of you."

I frown. "What, exactly, has Ev been saying about me that would make me being nice to a kid so surprising?"

"Nothing," he's quick to respond. "But not everyone gives random teenagers the time of day."

"Yeah, well, I don't think he gets the attention he needs at home. Not that his parents are neglectful or anything. But some of the things he's said have made me feel for him, y'know? Like I don't think his dad is super accepting of same-sex relationships and Joey—"

"Is as camp as a row of tents." Jack nods, then grimaces. "That sucks about his dad."

"Maybe he'll come around? Either way, I just feel like giving him a safe space where he can feel free to be himself is something easy that I can do. He's Mia's friend, and our home is always open to him. Plus," I feel my cheeks heat, "maybe I would have been quicker to accept my feelings for Ev if I'd had same-sex couples to talk to growing up. Not that my parents were anything like his dad...but I didn't know that for sure when I was his age." I scrub my hand over my face. "I don't know. I just feel for him."

"You're a good guy," Jack claps me on the back. "And, hey, I just had my own 'turns out I like guys too' moment not that long ago, so if you and Evan need back up, you can always call us."

It's a really nice offer and I grin, bobbing my chin. "Thanks, man."

"Also," he says as he finally makes his way towards his car, which is parked a few spaces up from mine, "you're welcome to come join our soccer team."

I scoff. "Hard pass. My dad bod is not built for sports."

Thankfully, Ev loves it anyway.

***

Raucous squeals and laughter emanating from down the hallway make me wince as I pull back the covers of my bed.

"This was your idea," Ev tells me with a smug smile, then closes the bedroom door, shutting out the worst of the sound. He peels off his shirt and tosses it to the floor, and I'm momentarily too distracted by his toned chest, and the still-pink scars from his accident and surgery, to get annoyed with his untidiness. He chuckles. "My eyes are up here, buddy."

"Shut up," I mutter, blushing at having been caught ogling him.

I feel a little guilty for the arousal coursing through me. It's not entirely my fault: we were exchanging orgasms at the rate of horny teenagers for months on end, and then they stopped suddenly during what we now refer to as the Week Of Doom. My balls are bluer than Marge Simpson's hair at this point. However, until Ev's given the all-clear from his doctor to resume physical activity, I'm not going to act on my building frustration.

It would just be nice if he'd stop being so fucking attractive.

"Do you like what you see, baby?" he all but purrs, sliding under the covers beside me.

I give him a look that reads 'are you stupid?' but I don't answer.

He sidles in closer, running his palm down my t-shirt-covered chest and stomach, then lower still. I suck in a breath as my cock realises what's happening and practically springs to attention.

"*Evan*," I hiss, trying for a tone of warning but sounding stupidly needy to my own ears. "Stop it."

"This" —he *squeezes* my erection through my boxers— "doesn't feel like you want me to stop."

"W-we can't."

"No?" He presses his shirtless form right up against my side and then mouths at my neck, trailing wet kisses over the curve of my jaw and to my earlobe. I *throb* for him. "Why not, baby?"

How does this man manage to make me feel like an inexperienced teenager so easily? Between his touch and his sinful voice, I could just erupt.

Oh, yeah, *weeks* of celibacy. That's how.

Trying not to whimper, I answer, "You're still recovering."

"Doc said that once I was allowed to walk around again, I could resume other low-impact activities." Ev sounds so proud of himself. "Including sexual activity. We've just gotta be slow," to illustrate his point, his hand slips under the waistband of my boxers and strokes me up and down at a leisurely pace, "and careful."

Breathing heavily, I close my eyes and arch into his touch. "Fuck."

"Shh," his breath ghosting over the shell of my ear makes me feel weak with need, "there are impressionable teenagers in the house. We have to be quiet."

As if they'd hear us over their laughter anyway.

"I've missed this," he continues to croon into my hear. "Missed your pretty cock. Missed your mouth. Missed your hands on me."

Resolve crumbling, I rock my hips into the rhythm he's setting with his fist.

"You want this just as badly as I do, don't you?" Ev's voice is barely a whisper, but it echoes in my brain and through my nerve endings. "I can feel it, baby. I can feel you getting even harder in my hand. Feel you leaking for me. God, I wish I could have you inside me again..."

"Fuck," I repeat myself, unable to find other words. "Fuck. *Fuck.*"

He chuckles. "I know," he agrees, still sounding so decadent and teasing, "But not tonight. I'm too wired." He moves, bracing his toned, nearly-naked body over mine, slotting a leg between mine and rutting his hard cock, covered only by the thin layer of his boxer briefs, into my thigh. "Feel it?" He asks. "Feel how hard you make me, baby? Feel me leaking for you?"

"I do," my voice sounds wrecked and gravelly and I can hear my own heartbeat in my ears. "I want...Ev...*please*..."

"What do you want?"

"N-naked," I demand through heavy, panted breaths. "I want to get naked. Both of us. I want..."

Why are words so difficult?

It could be because all of my blood is currently running directly to my dick, not leaving a lot behind to run my brain.

Speaking of my dick...

Evan is already halfway through helping me out of my shirt and, with some awkward manoeuvring, I help him finish the job, not caring when he chucks it off the side of the bed. Then he climbs off me to tug down my boxers and turfs those aside, too. While he's up, he wriggles out of his underwear, and then we're both stark naked, and I drink in the sight of him in the glow of the bedside lamp.

His skin glows golden under the warm, yellow light. He's just as toned and perfect as I remember, even with the faded bruising and the scars from his accident. His chest hair is a bit patchy from where they had to shave him for surgery, but it's still enough for me to tangle my fingertips in.

How did I ever convince myself I was straight?

Don't get me wrong: boobs are still awesome, but Ev's body is droolworthy. Plus, I'm so in love with him, it makes him even more attractive.

His cock, long and lean, bobs in the air as he moves back over the mattress and brackets himself over me again, this time with his legs on either side of mine, well and truly pinning me beneath him.

My breath catches at the feeling of skin on skin, of our cocks brushing against each other, of feeling completely vulnerable and also utterly wanted by the man on top of me. I run my hands up his sides, probably far too gently, but remembering his warning that we need to be slow and careful.

"*Shit,* Jay," he exhales and rocks his hips, whether because he's seeking friction or wants to get closer, I don't particularly care, "you feel so good."

"I haven't done anything yet" —he rolls his hips with a bit more force and the feeling of his cock rubbing up against mine is pure bliss— "*ah!*"

"Shh," he bends to press his lips to mine, all of his weight braced on his strong arms, his tasty biceps straining on either side of my head, "we've got to be quiet, remember?"

It feels completely different to be beneath him like this. Aside from the time he sat in my lap and rode me, I'm usually the one pretending to be in control. But tonight, I'm content to be passive. To let Ev set the pace and take the lead.

It feels surprisingly awesome to be underneath him. To be surrounded by him. To look up into his handsome face and imagine him pushing his way into my body the way I normally sink into his.

He pauses and sits up, fumbling in the nightstand for the lube. He squirts a generous amount into his palm and then coats our cocks with it, sitting back on top of my thighs as he jerks us together languidly. I watch his olive-toned hand work our dicks together, loving the way we just fit together so well. Precum pearls and leaks steadily from both of us, and I moan when he scoops some of the combined liquid up on his thumb and then pops it between his kissable lips, sucking noisily.

"*Jesus Christ,*" I exhale, "that was hot."

He grins and then stretches over me again, kissing me fiercely, coaxing my lips open with his tongue to share the flavour with me.

I whine low at the back of my throat at the sensory overload. "I'm gonna come," I warn him, blushing at how soon into this experience it's happening.

But it has been *weeks* and I am completely keyed up.

I feel him grin against my lips, but then he moves his mouth to the shell of my ear again, lowly encouraging me, "Come for me, baby. Come all over my cock."

I pant as the pleasure builds and crests, egged on with his command.

"That's it," his own heavy breathing only makes me chase the high more, "show me how much you like it."

"E-Ev..."

His hand tightens its slippery hold, and he jerks us together faster, leaning all of his weight on his other arm. "I've got you, baby. I've got you. Give it to me."

"Oh fuck," my hips jerk as I feel the tension inside me reaching breaking point, bursts of pleasure beginning to spark through my nerve endings, "fuck, Ev, *fuuuuuck.*"

My orgasm washes over me like a tidal wave and I'm swept away in it. I come and I come and I come, coating his hand, his cock, and our bellies in my release. I'm dimly aware of him stroking harder and faster, chasing his own release as he uses the evidence of mine as additional lube.

I'm still floating in the afterglow, my body trembling from the intensity of my release as Ev drops his head to my shoulder and practically sobs, "Yes, Jay...Jay...*James.*"

Hot splashes of fresh cum land on the mess already between us and I flinch away from his touch as I finally start to come down, my cock feeling hypersensitive and beyond spent.

Ev collapses beside me, one arm and one leg draped over me as our chests heave in unison and we catch our breaths. I turn my head to lazily kiss his sweaty forehead and he tilts his head back, begging for a real kiss.

It's lazy and sloppy and languid...and absolutely perfect.

"I love you," he murmurs when it comes to an end. He nuzzles his face into my shoulder and adds, "I've changed my mind. I was wrong. I want to move in."

My lips twitch with amusement. After all of his 'I'm being the rational one', and the serious chats we had about my impulsive offer, it's just like him to change his mind. I love that about him. I love that he's not afraid to admit he was wrong.

"Then move in," I tell him, not making a big deal out of his change in tune. I'm too happy to tease him. "You've practically been living here the past few months anyway."

Because I really am happier when he's here. We've already proven that our daily routines fit in easily with each other and, after almost losing him, it triggers my anxiety when he's *not* around. That's something I'm working through with my therapist because, yes, both he and Doctor Rogers were right about us needing one, especially after his accident, too. (See? I can admit when I'm wrong, too.)

"It's that easy?" he asks, sounding surprised. "Just like that?"

"Why wouldn't it be? Everything is just that easy with you."

It always has been.

Maybe that's another sign I missed over the years. Things with Ev have just been easy. We just make things work together. This isn't any different.

"You don't think it's moving too fast? I mean, I thought when we talked about it, you agreed that it was."

I consider that for a second, then shrug. Yes, he had convinced me that my offering (demanding?) for him to move in with me moments after he regained consciousness was probably a hasty, panic-fuelled suggestion, but it never stopped me from wanting him here with me.

Besides, we have done everything else arse-backwards anyway.

"We've spent our lives together already," I muse out loud. "Yeah, most of that was just as friends, but you're the person who knows me best in this world. You moving in isn't going to change the way we hang out casually, it's not going to change the way we feel about each other...well, not unless you insist on leaving your clothes on the floor..."

"I guess I can work on that."

"Then what difference will it really make? Other than being able to do this" —I bend to kiss him again, this time sweetly— "whenever I want."

See, everyone important in our lives knows about our relationship now. They even accept the fact that we're still wearing the tacky rings he bought as a prop, even though we're probably never actually going to get married. I've started meeting his soccer friends as 'the boyfriend', and I plan on introducing him to my work friends in the same capacity.

"I thought you'd be more freaked out by it, is all."

Hugging him closer, I shake my head. "I was more freaked out when I thought I was going to lose you."

"Jay..."

"No, listen. That put everything into perspective. Even Mia's pregnancy scare. Because all those fears I had about life changing, or about what people might think of me...they were *nothing* in comparison to the fear of not having you in my life, as my best friend or as my partner. Boyfriend. Lover. Whatever. And I promised myself that if —*when*— you got through surgery, I was going to make sure that I was just as strong and brave for you as you've always been for me. That's why I've gone to therapy. That's why I'm not allowing the fear of all the things that could go wrong to get to me. Because there are also so many things that could go right, too."

I feel his Adam's apple bob as he swallows. "That's...deep, Jay," he says playfully, but his voice is thick with emotion.

"I know. But I love you, Ev. I will always love you. So move in with me. And if you still want to talk about having kids one day—"

"Nope," he cuts me off, laughing as he sits up so he can shake his head emphatically. "Nope. *Nope.* That was a one-off offer for a hypothetical scenario. We can be kickass grandads together one day, if Mia ever does have kids. But...no. No kids. Just us and Mia."

Relief floods through me and I grin, sitting up as well. "That sounds perfect to me." Then I look down my body and scrunch up my nose. "But for now, let's grab a shower."

"Yeah," he waggles his eyebrows, "I could go a second round in the shower."

Before I can tell him that that's *not* what I meant, my best friend-come-boyfriend has climbed out of bed and raced into the ensuite. I snort to myself and follow him at a more leisurely pace.

If anyone would have told me that a crazy fake-engagement would lead to the most rewarding relationship of my life, I would have laughed in their face. I'm glad I went along with my daughter's harebrained scheme. And, though she still tells us it's weird, I think that, secretly, she's happy for us, too.

Epilogue

Evan – One Year Later

"**D**ads," Mia whines, "Joey's stolen my MAC lipstick again."

From where I'm chopping up salad veggies at the kitchen bench, I sigh, then lean towards the hallway and call back, "Joe, give it back! I'll take you shopping for your own on the weekend!"

"What happened to that whole 'no more kids' thing, again?" Jay asks from his spot on the other end of the counter, where he's seasoning the minced beef for the hamburger patties we'll be throwing onto the barbeque in a couple of hours. "Because I'm pretty sure we've got two now."

He's not entirely wrong. Joey has been staying over at our place more frequently lately. He came out to his parents at the start of the new school year and, while his dad didn't hurt him, his home life has been uncomfortable at best. Jay and I made it clear that our door is always open to him and, as such, he's practically moved in.

"Didn't Mia always ask for a sibling?" I ask, and James snorts.

"She asked for a little sister when she was five. I bought her one of those dolls that wets itself instead and the novelty lasted all of a week before she was asking if she could just have a puppy instead."

"Joe's kind of like a puppy." He's got the boundless energy of a golden retriever, anyway.

"He does sneak into her room and steal her things," he agrees. Then he cocks his head. "Since when do you know anything about shopping for makeup?"

While he's not actually our foster kid or adoptee, I've been treating Joey like he is because I know there's no way his parents would be okay with him exploring his interest in fashion and makeup. He has a wardrobe full of more feminine clothes (most of which I bought him to get him to stop pilfering from Mia's collection), and now we're going to work on expanding his makeup supplies.

"I don't," I admit. "But Jack's partner, Leo, is apparently good with it. Dolls himself right up."

I pull out my phone and bring up the photo Jack sent me of him and Leo on their last date night. In it, Jack's boyfriend's eyes pop with a splash of glittery eyeshadow and bold fake eyelashes, and his already sharp cheekbones seem even more striking because of whatever contouring he did. He's stunning, but not my type. I still prefer my men bigger, with blond hair and cuddly dad bods. "See? He's volunteered to come along. Said he'll even give Joey some lessons."

"Thank God," Jay breathes. "No offence, honey, but I was worried you'd end up making him look like a clown."

"I happen to know my own strengths and limitations, thanks," I tease back. "Unlike the time you took Mia formal dress shopping." Having my stepdaughter call me near tears because her dad was picking her the most conservative dresses he could find is an experience I will hold over his head for eternity.

He pouts. "I can't help it if I think women are sexy with a bit of mystery."

"You went into Neanderthal Dad mode and I had to rescue her."

"Oooh," Joey saunters in and steals a slice of cheese from the plate I've set aside, "are we talking about James' terrible fashion sense again?"

"I do not have terrible fashion sense," my boyfriend, bless his cotton-nylon blend socks, growls. "And don't eat all the food before we can turn it into dinner."

"Daddy James is mad," Joey stage-whispers to me, specifically to get a reaction.

James, naturally, doesn't disappoint. He groans. "Don't call me that. You know I hate it."

I shake my head, trying really, really hard (read: not trying at all) to mask my amusement. "You know he only does it because you react that way."

"When do you turn eighteen again?" James asks our not-actually-adopted kid. "Because once you're eighteen, you're officially an adult and will become Centrelink's problem."

"Dad, that's mean," Mia saunters into the kitchen, as if she hadn't just been whining about Joey stealing her things. "You won't kick him out." She reaches out and smooshes Joey's cheeks with one hand, forcing him into the whole 'duckface' pout. "Look at this face. You love him."

Joey gets points for just rolling with it.

"That's debatable," James mutters under his breath. I lob a chunk of onion at him. "*Hey!*" he complains. "No throwing food. One, it's a waste. Two, you'll be the one cleaning up." Then he reaches out and slaps Joe's hand away from the cheese. "And stop eating it all!" Turning to me he says, "It's like we never feed them."

"I'm a growing boy," Joey insists. He bats his lashes at us, trying to make himself look like the Puss In Boots gif, all pitiful and such. "Don't you want me to grow up big, and strong, and capable of finding a sexy man of my own?"

"Gross," Jay declares, scrunching up his nose. "I don't want to think about my kids' love lives."

"Ah ha!" Joe throws his hands in the air and then points both index fingers at James. "You *do* think of me as your kid."

"You're our bonus kid," I agree, while I watch Jay's expression flash through a number of emotions. He's gotten much better about handling changes, I'll give him that, but sometimes he still struggles with the sudden realisation of feelings. Like working out that he really does love our bonus kid, who isn't really ours but might as well be.

"Think about it this way, baby," I tell him when he still hasn't said anything, "you fed the stray puppy, and it followed you home, and now it lives here."

To be honest, I'm a little surprised that Joe's parents haven't realised who he's staying with ninety percent of the time. I was also surprised that the kid was still enrolled at Winchester, because I half expected that his dad would pull the funding, but Mia said that Joe threatened to post about it online and his dad decided that his own reputation meant more to him than destroying his gay son's senior year of high school.

Rich people are still so weird to me.

"I liked you better before you called me a stray, Ev," Joe sighs.

I shrug. "I just call 'em like I see 'em."

"Rude," he responds, then turns to Mia, "did you see who they cast as Sam in the musical?" He makes a face, then answers for her, "Freaking Scott Fairweather. It's like, *hello*, do you want the whole thing to flop?"

"Why are you complaining, though?" she asks him, then attempts to sneak another piece of cheese out from under Jay's nose. He swats her hand away, too. With a sigh, she turns back to Joe. "You got Harry, which is what you auditioned for."

"Only because I can do his part in tenor. I can't sing baritone to save my life." Sighing dramatically, he looks at me. "*Why* are all lead male parts always so...masculine? It's a *musical*. We're all gay." He holds up his hand to forestall James' rant about stereotypes. "I know, I know. I'm just venting. It's not my fault *I'm* a walking, talking cliché. I was born this way." He groans and points at me next. "Don't you dare start singing that Lady Gaga song."

I frown and, in an aside to Jay, complain, "You're right: he's been spending too much time here."

"Is it too late to put him up for adoption?" Jay plays along.

God, I love him.

"Oh, no. No, no, no, no." Mia snatches up the tea-towel from where it was tossed on top of the kitchen bench earlier and, with a swirl of her wrist, twists it in the air. Then she flicks her wrist and snaps the improvised weapon at me. "Bad. *Bad* Evvy. Stop making googly eyes at Dad. There are *children* present. Plus," she makes a face, "you'll spoil our appetites."

"Oh," I widen my eyes, feigning surprise and apology, "I am *so* sorry. I didn't realise!" Then, a split second later, my lips curl upwards and I set down my knife and turn to close the distance between myself and Jay. Wrapping my arm around his waist, I say, "I guess you'll *really* hate it if I do *this*."

Jay melts into the kiss, as he always does, and it quickly changes from being a playful act to a proper, decadent, loving kiss. The world around us fades into the background, and I'm just as lost in him as the first time we kissed.

Somewhere in the background, I can hear Mia making exaggerated gagging sounds, but it's interspersed with her laughter. She's actually really cool about our relationship, though she hates that we make it our life's goal to embarrass her in public wherever possible. Not in a negative way, but in a 'my parents are dorks, feel sorry for me' kind of way.

It's a lot of fun.

Of course, the bonus kid ruins it by loudly declaring, "*This* is why I stay here. Who needs porn when you get live shows?"

"Well, that's my libido dead forever," James declares as he steps out of my embrace. He points at the two miscreants on the other side of the kitchen bench. "You two can go set the table outside."

Mia rolls her eyes, while Joey smirks and says, "Yes, Daddy."

"Don't—" I start, but it's too late.

James makes an almost agonised, frustrated sound at the back of his throat. "Stop calling me that!"

I can't help but burst into laughter, and my boyfriend rounds on me with a scowl. "This bratty behaviour is all your fault."

"Mine? How?"

"Well, he's your kid."

"Uh…"

"Mimi's mine, and Joe is yours."

"That's not how it works, Jay."

"It is now."

Have I mentioned I love him? He's so ridiculous that it's adorable.

Jesus, I must love him because I just thought he was 'adorable'.

"Come on, hot stuff," I tease, and gesture to the bowl of meat in front of him. "Finish making the patties and I'll warm up the barbie."

"I hope you realise you're not getting laid for at least a week," he huffs.

"That's an idle threat. I give you two days before you're begging for a bj."

"Pfft. It'll be you begging."

I affect nonchalance. "We'll see."

(In the end? We last 24 hours by mutual agreement. Well, that's my story, and I'm sticking with it.)

Bonus Epilogue

James

"So, are you empty-nesters, yet, or is the demon child you unofficially adopted sticking around?" Leo asks me as we sit and watch our men on the soccer pitch.

While the social games they usually play are friendly, Jack and Ev decided to join a amateur competitive league, and their team made it to the finals of their first season. Naturally, their entire social team and their families and friends, Leo and I included, have come to watch the final game. As a group, over the course of the season, we've been playfully calling ourselves SPASM (Soccer Partners And Spouses Mostly), which always gets a rise out of our men.

"Demon child?" Toby asks from his seat in front of us.

I am familiar with most of these guys now, seeing as Jack and Leo have become good friends of ours, but there have been a few new faces today. Toby is one of them. He's in his late forties and looks every bit the typical Gold Coast surfer dude. His skin seems permanently tanned and is weathered by long hours in the sun. He's got thick, blond hair, and has an enviably athletic frame. It puts my beer gut to shame, that's for sure. But he's been very friendly and has come along with Jack's dad, Will, and his husband, Connor, who are also friends of Ev's.

"It's a long story," I sigh, shaking my head as Leo leans forward and says, "He's *evil.*"

"You only think he's evil because he flirts with Jack," I tell him, before looking back at Toby. "He's harmless. Just...forward."

"Uh huh," Leo folds his arms across his chest. "All I'm saying is now that he's eighteen, he's an adult and I will treat him as such."

Toby snorts. "Sorry to break it to you, but you're about as scary as a kitten wearing a tutu, Leo."

Leo sniffs. "I can't believe I taught that kid how to contour and then he goes and looks *prettier* than me."

"He doesn't look—no." I stop myself before I go down a rabbit hole I can't climb out of. "No, we're not going to objectify or belittle Joey when he's not here to defend himself."

Leo sighs. "Fine. That's fair." He cocks his head. "I'm mostly joking, anyway. Did he get into NIDA with Mia?"

Mostly joking. I want to laugh, but I manage to keep my composure.

"He didn't, no. But he applied to UNSW Sydney for a Bachelor of Fine Arts majoring in Visual Arts and Media...or something like that," I wince a little because I can never remember the exact name of his chosen degree, "and he got in, so he and Mia are going to share a place together with a couple of other students."

"That must be stressful for you," Toby says with empathy. He's been raising his daughter as a single dad, too, which we bonded over when we were first introduced. "I'll probably be a wreck when Vi moves out for uni."

"You've still got a handful of years before that's an issue," Leo responds. "But, yeah, it would probably be a huge change." He gives me a little smile. "But you've got Ev to keep you on your toes, at least."

"He's the biggest child of all of them," I agree. "With the kids moving out, he's started begging for a puppy."

Leo groans. "Don't let Huddy and Prez hear that. They've gotten sick of the cat and are back on the 'can we have a dog, Dad?' mantra."

"Oh dear," I commiserate, looking up at the pitch briefly as some of the spectators cheer. When I realise they're cheering for the other team, I switch my attention back to Leo, "how are you distracting them from that?"

"Well, Hudson's made a new friend at school this year. A little girl named Ava. He's absolutely smitten, and he wants to do gymnastics classes with her. I've told him that he can do that instead of having a puppy."

"And Preston?" I ask about Hudson's twin. "He's not interested in gymnastics?"

"No," Leo sighs. "He's going to be a tougher nut to crack. But, *oh*, get this: Ava's dad is some former big name soccer player from the UK. Jack went a bit starry-eyed when we met him. It was cute. But, anyway, he's apparently also the coach of the new Gold Coast soccer team. You know, the A-League one?"

"I...don't actually follow the soccer," I admit. "Ev's lucky that I love him enough to come watch him play."

Leo laughs and nods. "That's fair enough. I watch it, but I don't play it. But," he grins widely, "Ava's *stepdad* —yeah, I know, I was shocked, too, what with the whole soccer thing and all— her stepdad is the team captain."

I blink. "Is that even allowed?"

"Apparently. I mean, nepotism happens in sport all the time. This is pretty much the same thing."

Another cheer goes up and this time it looks like our team is close to getting a goal. We pause our conversation to watch the guys passing the ball and dodging the opposing players.

I have to admit, watching Ev run around all sweaty and in those shorts is actually kind of a turn on.

Then Ev gets the ball and passes it to Jack, then he makes a break towards goal and Jack crosses the ball back to him and Ev kicks it and *holy shit*, he actually gets it into the net, right over the goalie's outstretched hand.

I push to my feet and cheer, only barely stopping myself from yelling out a proud 'That's my man!' as the rest of us celebrate the point. When I check my watch and realise that there's only another five minutes left, plus whatever stoppage time, I even get a little excited that my boyfriend might even have scored the winning goal.

"That was a fantastic bit of footwork," Toby says, gesturing towards the pitch. "I can see why they switched up to the competitive games.

"I think their friend Brett basically begged them," I nod, now more invested in watching the last few minutes play out. "His team was short a couple of members."

"From memory, he's the really competitive one, isn't he?" Leo asks.

I nod. "Yeah. He's obsessed with soccer. I think Ev said something about him originally wanting to play professionally, but he didn't make it?"

"Hang on," Toby interrupts with a frown, then he squints at the pitch, "I think I know that Brett guy. I think his kid goes to the school I teach at." The way he says it does not sound complimentary. He looks back up at us. "The kid is great, but the dad's a dick."

"He didn't seem awful the couple of times I've met him," I shrug. "But it's not like we had long chats, either."

Toby shrugs. "Well, as long as he's nice to your guys. And to Connor. Hey, Con," he leans forward to talk to Connor, who is also on Jack and Ev's social team, "what are your thoughts on the guy with the ponytail?"

"Which one?" he asks, leaning forward. "That Neville guy? Or Brett?"

I scan the pitch and realise there is another guy with his long-ish hair secured on top of his head in what might be classed as a ponytail if you squint. I'd call it more of a man bun, personally. However, he can't be more than twenty-five if he was a day, and it's fairly obvious Toby isn't talking about him. All that aside, I do feel a bit guilty for not making more of an effort to get to know all the guys on the team. Leo obviously has.

Oblivious to my musings, Toby juts his chin in reply to Connor's question. "The older one. With the *actual* ponytail."

"Brett, then. Why?"

I tune them out as Toby launches into his 'small world, even smaller city' connection. I check my watch again and note that there are only a couple of minutes left on the official clock, and the other team haven't scored yet. I jiggle my leg anxiously. I've never been this invested in the outcome of a soccer game before.

When the whistle finally blows, I launch to my feet, cheering and clapping for the winning team —Ev's team— as they shake hands with the other team and then trail off the pitch.

We get out of our seats and head down to meet up with the players, who are guzzling from water bottles and wiping off sweat with gym towels. Not caring that my boyfriend is sweaty and gross, I launch at him, congratulating him for his goal.

"You're proud of me, huh?" he asks playfully, and I nod, grinning.

I'm aware of some of the others looking our way and, even though soccer has a reputation for being homophobic, I don't care what these men think. I'm riding on the high of watching *my* boyfriend win the game for them.

"It was hot. My boyfriend, the goal-kicker."

Out of the corner of my eye, I can see the young guy with the man-bun's lips quirk up into a little smile as he wanders past us. Something in the expression fleetingly reminds me of Joey, but then Ev's snort distracts me.

"Oh, I see how it is. Success turns you on, yeah?"

"Your success does, yeah."

To be fair, everything about him turns me on. We've been together for over eighteen months now, and I still feel like we're in the honeymoon period of our relationship. Honestly, though, I hope that feeling never fades.

"Well, I was gonna shower here, but maybe I'll shower at home instead." The words are accompanied by an eyebrow waggle. "Want to join me?"

I don't need to be asked twice.

***

"Fuck," Ev's fingers tighten in my hair as water cascades down over us. His voice echoes off the tiles, and I have never been happier that the kids are adults off living their own lives right now. "Baby, your mouth…"

I hum around his cock, now well-versed in how he likes to be sucked off. With a slippery finger (or three) teasing his hole, he basically turns into a whimpering puddle of a man.

"You're so good at that. So fucking good. I've created a monster," he babbles, alternating between fucking into my mouth or onto my fingers. "*God*, yes, there."

My knees are starting to hurt from being on the hard tile of the shower floor for a few minutes now, but I'm enjoying watching him unravel far too much to stop.

As if he can read my mind, he starts muttering, "Don't stop, don't stop."

I hum around the dick in my mouth, and crook my fingers just right.

"Oh, *fuck*, baby…"

I'd be quite happy for him to finish down my throat and then return the favour, but when he whines, "Get up here and fuck me properly", I can't refuse him.

Pulling off his cock with an audible 'pop', I let him help me back up to my feet and then he slams his mouth on mine, shoving me back against the shower wall. The shower spray continues to rain down on us, and our skin glides together with just the right amount of friction.

"Where's the lube?" I ask him when we part for breath.

He fumbles through the caddy for the little bottle and presses it into my hands.

"Swap places. Hands on the wall. Arse out," I command, swatting the very sexy backside in question for emphasis.

"Fuck I love it when you take charge," he tells me, and I grin, uncapping the bottle with a satisfying snap of the lid.

We ditched condoms not long after he was well and truly declared recovered from the accident, and I still don't think I'll ever get used to how amazing it feels to slide inside him. We both moan as my cock pushes in and breaches the rim, and then I take my time enjoying the warm, moist, tight clench of him around my cock as I inch all the way inside.

Reaching around him, I stroke his dick while I start to thrust, but I have a feeling I'm going to come before he does tonight. It's always a gamble, and neither one of us ever walks away disappointed in the end, but I still tend to feel more accomplished if I make him come first.

There's something about seeing and hearing him come undone that does it for me more than anything else. Given how my feelings for him started all those years ago, it's possible that that's always been my thing.

"God, I forgot how big you feel from this angle," he moans and sticks his butt out further, bracing his palms on the tiled wall. "Like you're going to make it to my damn belly button...*fuck*, yes, just like that."

I grip his hips and slam as deep as I possibly can, making the water cascading over us splash and slap.

"You always feel amazing around my cock," I pant, fucking in and out of him at an increasing pace. "So fucking tight. So hot.

And *this arse"* —I release one of his hips to squeeze a perfect, bronze-coloured globe— "fuck, it's perfect, Ev."

"Yes," he babbles with every thrust inside him, "yes, yes, *yes.*"

"You were so hot kicking that goal tonight," I tell him, "so hot running around out there in those —*nnnghh*— those clingy shorts. Showing off this" —I can't help smacking his butt cheek— "perfect fucking arse."

"Oh *god!*" he cries and slaps the tiles. "D-do that again."

"What?" I pant, because honestly I'm *this* close to blowing my load.

"Sm-smacking my butt. It felt—"

I slap the fleshy globe again, the sound echoing with the extra smack of the water between his cheeks and my hand.

"—*fuck, baby.*"

This is a new, but fun, discovery.

"Again?" I ask him and he nods.

I squeeze his backside before I smack it this time, and he arches his back and lets out an emphatic, "*Yes!*"

He clenches around my cock with the same movement and I can't smack him anymore because I'm practically going cross-eyed with pleasure. "Fuck, Ev. Fuck," I grunt, reaching the point of no return, "fuck, you feel so good. I'm coming. I'm —*nnnnghh.*" I grind into him, coming as deeply inside him as I possibly can, wanting him to feel me for days.

Then, once the initial buzz fades and my brain kicks back into gear, I spin him around, drop back to my knees, and finish him off with my mouth.

It doesn't take long for him to come, not with three of my fingers finding their way back inside him, using my cum for additional lube as I seek out his prostate and rub it over and over again.

With one hand yanking at the hair on my head and the other scrabbling for purchase on the slippery tiles behind him, he howls my name as he comes, pouring his hot release down my throat in a thick, rewarding wave of bliss.

Once he slips from my mouth, he slides down the wall to rest on the shower floor beside me.

We catch our breaths, and he swipes wet hair off my forehead, grinning. "I demand a reward like this for every game I win."

I snicker and lean forward for a sweet kiss, allowing him to taste himself on my tongue. "Mmm," I hum happily. "Seems reasonable to me."

It's not like I'm losing anything with that deal.

In fact, ever since he agreed to be my fake fiancé, it feels like all I've done since then is win.

The End.

***

Thank you so much for reading *A Match Made In Evan*. I giggled far too much while I wrote it, and I genuinely hope you enjoyed it.

I'd love it if you could leave a review on your retailer of purchase or wherever you read and write reviews.

Reviews not only tell the algorithms that our books deserve attention, but honest feedback also encourages and inspires me to keep writing. Even a star rating helps, and I greatly appreciate you taking time to do so.

Speaking of my writing, if you want a glimpse into Book Four of the Dads & Adages world, titled *Speak Of The Neville*, keep turning the pages because the first chapter is waiting for you.

Also, if you'd like to read about Will & Connor's wedding and honeymoon night (which functions as an extended epilogue for Book 1, *Where There's A Will*), you can subscribe to my newsletter and snag a copy at:

https://annasparrows.com/newsletter-subscription/

If you're already signed up and still want a copy, you can visit:

https://books.bookfunnel.com/annasparrowsbonus

to claim copies of the bonus content you don't yet have.

Please also consider following me on my socials at:

Website: https://annasparrows.com/

Facebook: https://www.facebook.com/AnnaSparrowsAuthor/

Instagram: https://www.instagram.com/annasparrows

...And now, without further ado, the sneak peek of *Speak Of The Neville* awaits!

Sneak Peek: Speak Of The Neville

Chapter One – Pete

"Uh, Pete?" My thirteen-year-old foster son, Mason, sounds concerned as he calls for me from the kitchen. "The, um, the kitchen is flooding."

From where I have *just* sat down in the living room to relax after a long shift at work, followed by cooking dinner for myself and the boys, I launch back up to my feet with a groan. My legs ache and my back protests.

I'm not unfit, but I'm definitely starting to feel the strain of my job. Then again, I am forty-three. Nearly officially in my mid-forties. *Ugh.*

"What do you mean the kitchen is—*fuck*." I come to a standstill in the entrance to the room in question, gaping at the water gushing out from under my dishwasher (which I only loaded twenty minutes ago) and covering my polished wooden floors.

Beside me, with his brown eyes wide as saucers, Mason quickly says, "I didn't do it."

"I know, bud," I assure him gently.

I've been fostering Mason and his older brother, Jack, for a few years now. Ever since my team of firefighters rescued them from a burning warehouse in Burleigh's industrial area, where they'd been squatting after running away from their separate foster homes because they wanted to be together.

That whole rescue was a disaster, but after the boys' story came to light, I called a social worker buddy of mine and threw my name into the hat as a volunteer carer for them. My job, as the Captain of the Burleigh Heads Fire Department, was a sticking point, given that I was —and still am— single and work unpredictable hours. However, with my sister offering to be available on nights when I'm not, I was granted foster custody by the time the boys were released from hospital.

The boys are good kids, but, even so, it has been a bit of a roller-coaster for all three of us over the past three years. Jack, being on the cusp of puberty when they first came to me, was angry and hyper-protective of his brother. And Mason was skittish and unused to affection from anyone other than Jack. Even now, after three years together, I still need to reassure Mace that he's in a safe space and not in trouble.

"I just came in here to get a can of Coke and found it like this," he hurries to add, ignoring my words entirely.

"No, I know, Mace. It's okay."

I curse myself for being so sharp as I came into the room, but even Mason's therapist has said that he needs to get used to people raising their voices around him in certain contexts. I'm not sure I agree entirely with his assessment, but I do have to acknowledge that the real world is a noisy, unpredictable place.

Still, I'm uncomfortable with simply expecting Mason to adapt or mask his reactions to meet the world's demands.

Even though he's thirteen, he seems younger. More sheltered and naïve. I love that about him. He thrives on routine and hates getting in trouble, and for the most part, that has been a positive thing.

Besides, his brother is enough of a trouble-maker for the both of them.

"Jack didn't do it, either," Mason tells me, as if that was going to be my next thought.

"Well, he's at Holly's place at the moment, so I couldn't blame him even if I wanted to," I answer playfully. Then, understanding that Mason is not in the right headspace to understand that I'm joking, I add, "Which I don't. Jack's not like that."

"Mister Tibbits probably would have blamed him."

"Yeah, well, that's because Mister Tibbits is a wanker." I actually hate the principal of the local high school.

Now, I thoroughly respect teachers and educators. My sister is a teacher at a primary school, so I have heard how tough the job can be.

But Arthur Tibbits is a judgemental, holier-than-thou, conclusion-jumping fuckwit. Any time there's any sort of disruption in one of Jack's classes, he's more than happy to lump the blame on my kid. He doesn't stop to ask questions or to get the full story, he just gives Jack a detention —or a suspension— and I get the call telling me to get my kid under control.

Mason's giggles tear me from my angry thoughts. "You should say that to his face. It would make Jack happy."

"It would make all of us happy," I grumble. Then I sigh and wade through the spreading puddle on my beautiful floors and yank the dishwasher door open, stopping its cycle.

More water, dirtied from the mess on the dishes, sloshes out over my feet.

"Gross," Mason declares. When I turn around, I find that he has climbed onto the kitchen bench to peer across the space at the carnage. "Can you fix it?"

"I don't even know what's wrong with it," I admit. "I deal with fires. This is the complete opposite."

Mason looks at the clock on the wall and brushes his mop of dirty-blond hair off his forehead as he frowns. "Do plumbers even work at eight o'clock?"

"Emergency plumbers do," I nod. "Do you have your phone?" I left mine on the couch and I'm not trudging my wet feet over the nice, relatively new carpet to get it.

Mason nods and fishes the device —his most prized Christmas present— from his pocket.

"Can you Google local emergency plumbers?" I ask him, while I take the opportunity to open the cupboard under the sink and turn off the water. "I can call if you're not comfortable talking on the phone."

His smile is grateful and he types at his screen and then, after I slosh the three steps over to the kitchen bench, he hands me the device with his findings.

I click on the first link I find and then press the green call icon to connect to the number associated with the listing. A chirpy sounding receptionist takes my details and tells me she'll send 'one of the boys' out to help ASAP.

My bank account quietly cries about how much an emergency plumber is going to cost on a Sunday night, but this isn't the kind of thing that can wait.

"I guess we should start mopping this mess up while we wait," I say as I hand the phone back to Mason, and he scrunches his nose.

Good kid though he might be, he's still a teenager and, like all teenagers, he's allergic to chores.

"I'll give you ten bucks for Robux or whatever game it is you're currently addicted to." I am not above bribery.

Mace springs into action, presumably heading to the laundry to get the mop and bucket. I shout after him to get extra sponges, too. "The thick ones we use to wash the car!"

***

When the doorbell rings at half-past nine, I've already sent Mace up to bed. Jack came home twenty minutes ago, just after his curfew, but I let it slide because his girlfriend's mum texted to tell me that he was helping her clean up the mess her toddler, Holly's little brother, made during playtime.

I am a mess when I get to the door. My jeans are soaked from kneeling on the wet floor to sponge up what the mop couldn't, and I'm sweaty and grimy, but at least the kitchen floor has been saved from water damage. Well, I hope it has. I may need to get someone out to inspect it, just in case. The last thing I need is for the floors to warp, or for a mould problem to pop up out of nowhere.

Swinging the door open, I am not prepared for just how attractive the man on the other side of the doorway is. He's about my height, lean, but with biceps that suggest his t-shirt is hiding an enviably toned frame, and dark brown eyes so soulful that I almost lose myself in them for a moment.

I have got to get laid, I berate myself, especially when I take in more of the details of the plumber's very pretty face. He's young. Too young for me. But his short beard is trimmed with meticulous precision, framing a jawline and cheekbones most models would kill for. And his lips...

Fucking focus, Pete.

"Hi," I greet the young man lamely, then step back and run my hand through my greasy hair. I grimace at the feel of it, suddenly even more aware of how gross I must look. "Sorry, come on in. I'm a bit of a mess at the moment."

The plumber smiles, flashing a row of straight, pearly white teeth, and shrugs. "Most people are when they call us." He pats his chest, gesturing to his embroidered name tag. It reads 'Neville'. He does *not* look like a Neville. "Nev," he introduces himself. It's a better fit than Neville, that's for sure. Not that I can talk. There's a reason I go by Pete instead of Peter. "Now," he continues, cocking his head, "Trish said something about your kitchen flooding?"

"Yeah, this way," I close the front door and lead him down the hallway from the living room to the kitchen at the back of the house. "I loaded the dishwasher as usual and then, next minute, the kitchen is flooding. I've switched off the water under the sink, and I've mopped up the mess, but I had no idea what else to do from there and, obviously, we're going to need the water running again in the morning..."

Nev nods as I ramble, then carefully places his toolbag down beside the dishwasher. I brace myself as he pulls the door down to open it, but we're not met with a wall of water intent on undoing all of my cleaning up. I heave a sigh of relief as he peers into it and then moves around to open the cupboard under the sink.

"Ah," he says after poking around for a minute, while I do everything in my power to *not* check out his butt, "I think your hose has cracked."

My hose is doing something...

I wince and clear my throat. "Sorry, what?"

"Your dishwasher hose," he repeats slowly. "I think it's cracked."

"Oh. Is that...an easy fix?"

He smiles brightly and nods, and it's only now that I realise he is on his knees and eye-level with my crotch and I *really* need to stop perving on the *boy* the plumbing company sent to me.

Thankfully oblivious to my thoughts, Nev answers, "It's easy, and it's not that expensive." Those dark eyes take in the recently renovated kitchen and I know what he's thinking. A house in this condition, of this size, in Burleigh? I must be a multi-millionaire.

He'd be wrong, of course. I bought this place when it was a dated disaster of a house, barely good enough to be a shell for the home I envisioned. I paid what I thought was too much for it even then but, ten years later, property prices here on the Coast have boomed and, if I sold it now, I could probably buy three little houses in Brisbane and still have cash to spare. That's not going to happen, though. I like living near the beach.

Still, I just nod and thank him. "Can you fix it now?"

He grimaces and my heart sinks. "Unfortunately, no. I've gotta get the parts. But you're safe to turn your water back on in the meantime. The sink and dishwasher run on separate plumbing lines." I hadn't known that. I feel a little dumb for turning the water under the sink off. Nev keeps talking, "Just don't run the dishwasher. I'll help drain out the stuff that's left in the bottom of it so it doesn't go all stagnant and gross, though."

"Thanks."

I leave him to it, not wanting to hover (or drool) while he works. When he's done, he finds me in the living room and hands me a business card with his name on it and a mobile number underneath it. "Text me," he says, and I blink.

"I...what? You're a bit young for me, but—"

"What?" His voice goes up an octave and his cheeks turn a little pink. "Shit. No! That wasn't a come on. Sorry, I sometimes get a bit lost in thought and don't realise I haven't said half of what I was thinking."

Well, now I'm embarrassed. "Sorry, I..."

"No, no, that's my fault. I was thinking about how I'll get the parts tomorrow or Tuesday and then if you want to text me your number so we can arrange a time for me to come back and fix the dishwasher..."

I feel like an idiot. I will never, ever be able to look this man in the eye again. Nevertheless, I pull out my phone and text the number on the card. His phone trills in his pocket.

"For what it's worth," he says as I awkwardly shuffle him back out the front door. The sensor light comes on as he steps down onto the little stepping-stone path I set into the lawn not long after I moved in. The yellow of the light glints off his dark hair and eyes, making him somehow even more attractive.

I am a sucker for punishment.

"Yeah?"

Nev tilts his head and his plump, inviting lips tick upwards into a little smirk. "I don't think you're too old for me."

Then he spins on his heel and hurries down the path and to the van parked on the curb.

I'm still staring dumbly into nothingness long after the van has pulled away and driven off into the night.

About the Author

I am a bi Aussie author living in Brisbane, Australia. I've been writing* for as long as I can remember. I started with silly short stories as a kid, moved on to fanfiction in my teens, and then to publishing original fiction in my thirties.

I have been an avid reader of MM romance my whole life. (Ask me about my beginnings with *Buffy* fanfic, haha!) I wrote a sweet and kinky MM romance novel in 2022 and the reader response changed my life. From there, I knew I had found my niche.

And thus Anna Sparrows was born.

*All of my writing is 100% my own. No part of it is generated by Artificial Intelligence (AI) software of any kind. Yes, that means that it's sometimes flawed, but I'm okay with that.

Follow Me

Website: https://annasparrows.com

Facebook: https://www.facebook.com/AnnaSparrowsAuthor

Instagram: https://www.instagram.com/annasparrows

Newsletter: https://annasparrows.com/newsletter-subscription

Also by Anna Sparrows

I write ridiculously sweet & steamy MM romance with guaranteed HEAs...and sometimes with a side of kink. My backlist can be found at annasparrows.com

Littles & Lace Series

The Littles & Lace series is an MM Age Play series, following a group of like-minded friends in the BDSM community. You'll find mild ABDL, light Pet Play, Femme Play and more here.

Book 1: Asher's Answer

Book 2: Matteo's Mettle

Book 3: Ted's Temerity

Book 4: Spencer's Satisfaction

Book 5: Chance's Choice

Book 6: Josh's Jackpot

Dads & Adages Series

Visit Australia's sunny Gold Coast where an assortment of single dads find love and even learn a few life lessons along the way.

Book 1: Where There's A Will

Book 2: You Don't Know Jack

Book 3: A Match Made In Evan

Book 4: Speak Of The Neville (release TBA)

Related: A Surprise For The Holidays

Written in 3rd person POV, *A Surprise for the Holidays* is a sweet, fluffy MM Christmas novella with a grumpy former soccer player turned coach, a golden retriever younger player, and a precocious little girl. Featuring an Aussie Christmas, grumpy/sunshine vibes, an age gap and sand where you're used to snow, this novella brings additional heat to the festive season in more ways than one!

Shifters Sanctuary Series

In a world where alphas are thought to be extinct, a number of men are about to have their worlds rocked.

Book 1: His Alpha Unlocked

Book 2: His Prodigal Alpha

Book 3: His Unicorn Alpha (release TBA)

Down Under Daddies Series

Set in rural Western Australia, come meet the and the kinkiest and queerest band of stationhands any outback cattle station has ever seen.

Book 1: A Stable Daddy

Kinks & Conundrums Series

A spin-off from the Littles & Lace series, this series follows Daddies, Doms, Littles, and Pet Players as they discover their kinks and find love.

Book 1: Anson's Awakening